I HAVE TO TELL SOMEONE!
Please, please listen,
and be understanding of me . . .
at least be compassionate.

How am I ever going to tell Mom?
Will she cry? Will she scream?
Will it break her heart?

I AM SICK AND SCARED AND TIRED . . .
Ohhhhhhh I am sooooooooo scared,
so white-knuckled, heart in my throat,
head throbbing like it's going to explode
SCARED.

IT CAN'T BE HAPPENING TO ME!
But it is happening to me and
I've got to face it.
I'M PREGNANT.

OH, SOMEBODY PLEASE, PLEASE HELP ME!

Other Avon Flare Books Edited by
Beatrice Sparks, Ph.D.

ALMOST LOST:
THE TRUE STORY OF AN ANONYMOUS TEENAGER'S
LIFE ON THE STREETS

IT HAPPENED TO NANCY:
A TRUE STORY FROM THE DIARY OF A TEENAGER

Annie's Baby

The Diary of
Anonymous,
A Pregnant
Teenager

edited by Beatrice Sparks, Ph.D.

AN AVON FLARE BOOK

AVON BOOKS, INC.
1350 Avenue of the Americas
New York, New York 10019

Copyright © 1998 by Beatrice Sparks, Ph.D.
Published by arrangement with the editor
Visit our website at http://www.AvonBooks.com
Library of Congress Catalog Card Number: 98-92413
ISBN: 0-380-79141-2

First Avon Flare Printing: July 1998

AVON FLARE TRADEMARK REG. U.S. PAT. OFF. AND IN OTHER COUNTRIES, MARCA REGISTRADA, HECHO EN U.S.A.

Printed in the U.S.A.

The PAST will forever be a part of my PRESENT as well as my FUTURE.

—Annie

Foreword

Dear reader:

I suspect you think that Annie's problems are not your problems, that there is no way you would allow a boy to control your life . . . your entire future! But . . . whoa . . . wasn't that exactly the way

> "ANONYMOUS ANNIE
> 14 years old and pregnant"

felt before she met Danny?

We should all love and respect Annie for consenting to share her most private thoughts and experiences in the hope that they will help you make wiser decisions in your life, FOR THE DECISIONS ARE UP TO YOU! I can't make them for you, your parents can't, your teachers can't, all the king's horses and all the king's men can't! ONLY YOU! It is an *awesome responsibility* but I'm smiling, for Annie assures me *you* can do it! I know you *can*, too!

—Dr. B. (Beatrice Sparks)

I can't believe I woke up this morning and it was an ordinary day: Take a shower, brush my teeth, clean my room, slap a last-minute polish on my (due yesterday) science paper, do the breakfast dishes, empty garbage, etc. . . . then WOW . . . WHAMMY . . . CRASH . . . BANG . . .

Me! Limping off the soccer field all smelly and bruised and battered and stuff after my Volkswagen bug-diesel-truck collision with Mountain Marion Martin. I was streaked with grassy dirt, trying to push my sweaty, limp hair out of my face, and rubbing a big "owie" under my right eye. Actually, I was feeling generally like Humpty Dumpty, when HE . . . came running toward the football field, suited up like a regular NFL star and gorgeous as Brad Pitt, even gorgeouser . . . is that a word? If it isn't, it should be!

Anyway, he ground to a stop right in front of me like an airplane coming down the runway for a landing and said, "Hi. Should I ask how you're doin'?" Ordinary me looked around to see who he was talking to. He tapped my shoulder and started laughing. I couldn't help laughing with him. Usually I'm . . . you know, really uncomfortable around boys, except the guys who are my buddies, male slugs I've grown up with. But him! Wow! *Now* I guess I know what hormones are!! They seemed like a strange idea in health class, but then and there—KA-POWIE—I felt like a stick of dynamite had blown up inside me.

I remember every word the gorgeously gorgeous one said. Actually, they are each *forever* engraved in my memory and mind for posterity! He said, "I'm new here, and . . . I'm looking for a friend. A sort of, not embarrassed to be"—he snickered—"sweaty, sporty sort of friend." He looked past my grungy, stringy bangs into the very deepest part of my heart and brain, and my whole body and soul smiled back at him.

The guys on the field began yelling. As he ran off, he whispered very slowly, in a kind of husky whisper, as though it were a sacred secret, " 'Bye, friend."

I'm lying here on my bed going over and over and over the awesomeness of it all. HE wants *me* to be *his* friend! I want to be! I really do want to be! More than I've ever wanted anything in the world in my whole life!

September 12, Tuesday

6:32 a.m.

I got up before it was even light outside—(me! Who sometimes doesn't even hear my alarm clock go off)—showered, washed my hair and curled it on hot rods, used some of Mom's face mask, and tried on everything in my closet. I've got to look my very best today! I know *he said* he wants a "sweaty, sporty sort of friend," but I'm sure he wants a girl who sometimes looks like a girl's supposed to look too, at least I hope with all my heart he does. Oh please, please make him *not* want to see me looking my sweaty, dirty tomboy worst like he did last time.

4:21 p.m.

All day long, every time I had a chance, I prowled up and down the halls hoping I'd see *him* somewhere, but it's a big school. I wonder if *he's* been looking for me? Maybe going down the East hall while I'm going down the West one. (I can't believe I don't even know his name.) Maybe he's sick or was in an accident or something! That's dumb!

Wasn't that a crazy dream last night when I visioned us playing tennis together and *me letting him win*! Not likely! Mrs. Raynor says if we had a team here at middle school, I'd for sure be its captain.

Ummm . . . I wonder if I *would* let *him* win because of the hormones and the macho thing?

And . . . I guess I might as well face it; maybe he says to every girl what he said to me. I couldn't bear that! But I guess I could; maybe I'll have to. Ouch! That really hurts! It hurts, but it *could* be reality too. Goodness knows it happens often enough on TV and I've never really had a boyfriend before. I mean, no one ever seemed to like me *that* way . . . maybe it's *just* the way *I* want *him* to like *me*.

6:59 p.m.

Jenny called. She and Deanna were going to the mall, but I said I didn't feel like it. I'd rather just sit here and feel sorry for myself. I wish I hadn't told her how mushed I am about *him*. It makes me seem like a real nutcase, nerd, dweeb. Besides I wanted to *just happen* to rollerblade past the deserted schoolfield and the park and stuff . . . just in case . . .

I was out for about an hour and a half but no sightings. Poor me.

September 14, Thursday

4:42 p.m.

I'm trying to get over him. But it's not really getting over him! It's kind of like it was a dream or movie, or some other repeating and repeating stupid, idiotic thing. I can't believe something like this can make me feel so completely world-shatteringly, darkly empty.

September 19, Tuesday

4:17 p.m.

I used to write almost every day. Now there doesn't seem to be anything worth writing about.

September 21, Thursday

4:50 p.m.

Radder than rad news! Molly and I were coming off the soccer field, pushing each other and being silly, when I felt someone come up behind me and put their hands over my eyes. My heart literally flopped; I wanted it to be *him* so much, but I thought it was probably Mel or one of the other guys in one of my classes. But it *was* him! It was!

He took my shoulders and turned me around. "Hi, friend."

I blubbered back, "Hi, friend."

The world started turning in a completely different orbit as *he* told me his name was Daniel, but I should call him Danny, and that he'd been looking for *me* all week. It was like we were the characters in the Indian story *Ramona*, our paths almost crossing but just barely missing, at least for the longest week in my life. Both of us looking for each other like our lives depended upon it. At least that's how I felt.

Danny asked if I wanted a ride home after school. IMAGINE *me* in the raddest boy in the world's 1982 red Mustang convertible—just him and me! I still have trouble breathing just thinking about it.

The *bad part* is that he had to bring me home, drop me off, and get right back to work. Oh, I guess I didn't tell you that his dad bought the Four Seasons Restaurant on the corner of Hill and Elm. It's the really classy place with a huge waterfall in the entrance. Anyway, the *best part* is, he asked me to go to a movie Saturday. Isn't that the coolest, sweetest, most awesome thing that has ever happened in creation? Mom would die if she knew, but what she *doesn't know* won't hurt her.

September 22, Friday

4:29 a.m.

I can't wait! I can't wait! I can't wait! I prowled the halls like a banshee between classes, but Danny has become part of the air I breathe or something, and invisible. I'm scared witless that I won't be able to talk to him when we do have some time together! I'm such a "duh" sometimes, especially around boys. Especially boys I like. Especially a boy I really, really *like*.

Danny's dad must be superrich to give him his own sweet convertible, as well as to buy the restaurant and big old Pederson house on the river. He said his parents are divorced, and his mother lives in New York. She's probably someone beautiful, powerful, and famous.

My dad just grayly disappeared after their divorce when I was five. The only thing I vividly remember about him is my mom telling my aunt once that he "moved from job to job to job looking for money like a bee flits from flower to flower looking for honey." I remember thinking about that a lot.

Mom and I are both *so ordinary*, everyday, like everybody else. Maybe I'll seem too ordinary, everyday, and like everybody else to him. I don't want that! I want him to think I'm very, very special! Like a princess or a movie star or a . . . I don't know . . . I just want to be *more* than *plain me*! Could *plain me* possibly be good enough for *awesome him*? I do, do, do, do hope he will like me when he gets to know me. Will he? I'm not all that pretty, and I'm not all that smart, and our apartment is nice, but it isn't like the big old Pederson house. Hmm, well, I was *the attending Rose princess* at last year's Rose Festival. Does that count?

Be quiet my shivering, insecure heart. Like Aunt Martha told me once: "We're worth what we think we're worth in life, and if we think we're worth two cents people will treat us like we're worth two cents!" I'm worth a whole lot more than that! Especially to my mom, who has to have good sense to be chosen the teacher of the year at her high school, so there, little nobody, no self-confidence person!

Well . . . ah . . . just to be sure Mom doesn't find out, maybe I better meet Danny in the mall, at the Gap, where Sally, my neighbor, works. I know everybody there and they treat me like *I'm special*, even when I don't buy anything. That should be cool and impress him. Hey, wait a minute; either he'll like me *for me* or not at all. Right?

But . . . mmmm . . . maybe it would be best to call Danny at the restaurant and tell him to meet me at Jenny's. Mom would have a dizzy-fizzy if she thought . . . you know . . . she's soooo old-fashioned. She thinks fourteen-year-olds are babies, and that at middle school we ought to still be playing in sandboxes and making mud pies. Jenny's mom is much, much more open-minded; at least she is when she's home, which is practically never.

4:40 a.m.

I'm so excited, I can't sleep and I *must*. I can just see Danny picking me up, and I'll have these humongous dark circles under my eyes and red eyes like a vampire. Uggg, not that! I've got to look and act and be my very, very, very, very best! So good night dear friend diary.

P.S. I've never been soooo happy in my whole life!!! Guess what makes me sooooo happy—*Him!!* *Danny!* I love that name.

11:41 p.m.

You can't even imagine what a wonderful, marvelous, rad, joyous, sweet, happy time I had with Danny. He's not like any other boy I've ever dated. Ha . . . that's funny because I've *never* had a date before. Oh, I've walked through the park with Jerry Mills and gone skating with Bon and her two brothers and stuff but . . . well . . . this was like . . . like life on another planet in another sphere. Honestly, you can't even imagine how glorious it was.

I wasn't the least bit scared or tense or anything from the very first. Because HE made sure I wouldn't be. He came to Jenny's door, and at first I felt weird, like I was strung tight as my tennis racket or something. Then he looked right into my eyes . . . and heart . . . and said, "Hi, fellow sports nut. You look yummy and nummy out of your wrinkled, sweaty uniform."

I opened my mouth and my brains fell out. "And . . . you smell sweet for a change."

He punched me gently on the shoulder and laughed. "It's Ralph Lauren's latest, 'Old Tennis Shoes' cologne."

For some crazy-mixed-up reason that made me feel comfortable as a warm, curled-up cat being petted. And talking to him wasn't hard either. But maybe that was because he, thank goodness, did most of the talking. Oh, you would love him Diary, honest you would. He's had such a hard, miserable life. I thought *he had everything* important. The beautiful house so big it looks like a castle, and the lawns and gardens like a park, and his successful dad, and his sweeter than sweet car! But he's taught me that *things* aren't everything! Parked up by Pebble Creek, he told me secrets that no one else knows. He said he needed someone like me to talk to. I was so flattered, I thought I was going to melt. He confided in me that he's *sixteen*! And he's over a year behind in school because two years ago he was in a horrible car accident. He was in a coma for two whole months. Then he was in traction and rehab for two more months. I just cried and cried when he told me, and we hugged each other like two little lost kids. I felt so honored that he would share his pain with me, and I know that it was good for him to have someone to unburden his soul upon.

He called me an "Earth Angel." And I think I'm going to commit myself completely to being *just that* for him, no matter what!

I'm *so* glad I lied to Mom about going out with him. I know I shouldn't be, but she's strong and mature and all that, and doesn't need a support system like Danny does. We got a dose of the support system importance in mental health class, and I'm grateful for that because now I'll be able to support Danny, at least some. Honestly, I *do* feel kind of bad about lying to Mom, but I know she wouldn't understand me and Danny "bonding" so quickly. That's another mental health class word, and *age has nothing* to do with "bonding," no matter what she or anybody else thinks.

I know this sounds completely out-there in the cosmic-cosmic since I've only talked to Danny at school and on the phone and been out with him once, but always and forever, I will be concerned about him, even when I'm old and gray and I have children and grandchildren and great-grandchildren; even if he marries someone else, and I marry someone else.

I will remember *after death* the wind blowing through my hair and Danny's strong arms holding me so close, I was almost part of him. He said I warmed up the "hurting coldness" in him that he'd always felt before. *That* made the little bright smolderings in my heart *flame* brighter and brighter, and made them feel righter and righter! *I know* that's not grammatically correct, but it *was all right* and RIGHT! And it made *then*, and makes *now*, perfect sense to me! That's all that counts! No matter what Mom or anyone else says!

Our *particular spot by the side of Pebble Creek*, with the full moon filtering through the leaves, making lacy patterns on everything, will ever be special to me . . . no, not special, SACRED, in some, I can't explain, way!

We didn't . . . go very far . . . but . . . everything in creation seemed . . . like new . . . and wonderfully US and right and kind of . . . forever together, unbreakable, unshakeable!

We missed the whole movie, but actually, in a way *we were* a movie as we talked and walked along the side of our winding little stream. Twinkling stars sagged through the velvet black night watching over us. We threw rocks in the water to see their silver splashes and chased each other, often falling down in the meadows of sweet grasses and flowers. Once Danny climbed a tree and played Tarzan while I played Jane. It was amazing how free and completely unrestricted and "really me" I felt.

I know I can help Danny. I want to so much. He needs to heal from all the agony he's suffered. To feel well and safe again. I *know* I can help him by just always being there for him and for *always* being, as Mom says, his "EGO BOOSTER!" Who would ever have thought that big jock Danny would ever need simple, ordinary old Annie me?

The fact that he's over a year behind in school is very hard on him, I'm sure. He didn't mention it, but I just know some macho inner part of him feels . . . I don't know . . . kind of embarrassed or hurt . . . but it will be better now because I'm going to dedicate my life to helping him know that he's all the wonderful, marvelous things he is! At last, and for a change, Mom's teachings and preachings about the importance of self-confidence are going to come in handy.

I don't want *anything* or *anyone* to ever hurt him again. And I'm soooo glad we got distracted and didn't go to the movie.

2:14 a.m.

I just had a miserable, horrible nightmare dream of dear Danny struggling to stay upright in his "walker" and going through excruciating therapy as he tried to rebuild his shattered life. I vow ... I *really do* deeply and sincerely vow that in the future I will do everything possible to make him feel forever important, powerful, and loved. We won't be like the other silly, dweeby couples around school. We'll be truly special, because of his tragedy, especially because of the very, very specialness of *his* sharing his tragedy with me.

Sorry I'm wetting your pages with tears, dear Diary, but I can't help it.

"Oh sleep take me into thy loving arms that I may dream of my newfound love."
>   Annie William Shakespeare
>   A++++ student in Miss Turner's
>   composition class

(I wish)

4:21 p.m.

Sorry I haven't talked with you for a while, but it's like part of the time I'm a different person on a different planet in a different sphere. I know that sounds kadoodley, but it's really how I feel . . . it's like . . . well, for instance, Danny and I had lunch together and the regular cafeteria turkey and noodles tasted like the ambrosia of the gods (Mom's expression for the tastiest of the tasty). After lunch Danny teased me because I don't want Mom to know about him. He does that because it kadoodles me so much. Danny loves the word "kadoodle," but it's so childishly silly, I try not to use it. Sorry to say, it slips out anyway, and for some reason it always makes us crack up and laugh like two loony balloonies. I'm making up my own words again.

After lunch we walked outside and Danny teased me about the movie we saw last night when we should have been at the library studying. I could barely remember it—I'd been so enraptured by his presence! Actually, I *really* remember it all, *but vaguely*. At least everything is vague except the guy literally filling the girl's room with roses. Why do I remember that part so perfectly and precisely that

I can even, at this moment, smell the fragrance of the roses surrounding me, enveloping me, smothering me? I know this sounds corny and hopelessly hokey, but you know how Mom is always encouraging me to be "verbally picturesque." Her phrase; not mine, remember? She's told me a million-hundred times that the way to become the writer I want to become is to, every time I take pen or pencil in hand, paint a word picture, right?

It's a little hard to do in math—but what isn't hard to do in math? For me anyway.

Hey, as an about-to-be-great writer I'm sure messing up this entry to the max, aren't I? I know that should be "am I not" but it sounds sooooooo snooty when I say it or write it. Still I guess I'm glad Mom pushes me in the writing directions, or at least I will be when I get older and really try to write for money. Imagine making money doing something you like . . . no, LOVE TO DO!

Whoa . . . back up some. How did I get from a room filled with red roses to here? Guess I got so caught up in words that I almost forgot trying to make sense. So! Back to the rose thing. After lunch when Danny and I stretched out on the grass under the library window. It was warm and the tree-leaf shapes and shadows were like a lacy covering snuggling over and around us. Lazily, Danny began telling me about football practice, then suddenly stopped, reached way up over his head and picked a huge sparkling dandelion that was poking out from a crack in the old cement foundation. Gently and slowly, like it was the most precious gift in the world, he handed it to me. "Someday I'll fill every corner of your room with red roses, but for now I can give you only . . ."—he looked at the dandelion as though it were a magnificent yellow jewel—"this."

Our hands met. "It's greater, more beautiful, more precious than *anything* in the world," I said as I put it between our two faces, which were slowly coming together. The little yellow bloom seemed to expand until it touched both his lips and mine. "It's our *very own* private sun, in our *very own* private universe," I whispered.

"Our sun, our universe," Danny whispered back as he kissed me.

His kiss carbonated my every blood cell as both the red and the white ones exploded in my body in a manner totally unknown to me before. It was such a secret, sacred experience that I'm surprised that I am even now able, after all my unsure rambling, to share it with YOU!

It was a quiet, quick, gentle little kiss because there are snipes and snitches and eyes and mouths all around our private school, but it was still an experience I will remember with a lovely shuddering all the days of my life. Surely other kids don't feel *this* way! They couldn't!

10:03 p.m.

I've been standing at my window looking at the full, full moon and the glittering, sparkling stars surrounding it. I am like one of those stars. And Danny is my moon. How I wish I was a brilliant poet like Elizabeth Barrett Browning and could write the things of my heart to him. When Mom first read her poems to me, I thought they were dumb, dumb, dumb. How wrong I was, or maybe just not then able to understand the language of love. It is like a new language, a new expansion of life. How fortunate I am to now be entering into its new world.

> Oh sleep
> How I hate to fall into thy arms
> And cease the beauty of my thoughts of him
> Perchance I'll dream about
> His hand in mine.
> A dream divine
> A dream divine.
> Good night, sweet Prince.
> My first of endless poems all meant for thee.

September 28, Thursday

4:27 p.m.

I saw Danny only for a minute today. He had to go meet his father for lunch about some stupid thing, then he had a meeting with Mrs. Bowers and football practice and work and something else idiotic. He did however bring me a very, very, very, special, special gift! Guess what it was? Oh come on, guess. I can't tell anybody else in the world except *you* because it's so . . . personal and private . . . so *us!*

Okay, I know how much *you* want to know! It was one of the little matchboxes they use to light candles in their restaurant, BUT squished inside were four little *chocolate kisses!* Isn't that about the sweetest, dearest, most thoughtful, original thing you've ever heard of? Almost better in a way, and more thoughtful than a whole room full of roses, or even dandelions.

September 29, Friday

9:22 p.m.

Danny and I were just beginning to eat our lunches when Bruster and Kel whirlwinded by our table and took him off. He shrugged and gave me a sad little look. I didn't see him the rest of the day. I know he works most nights at the restaurant, but I wish he'd phone.

> By the phone
> All alone
> All alone
> By the phone.

What I'm thinking now is really crazy, but since I've known Danny I sort of feel *alone even when I'm*

19

with other people. Insane, right? Right! But it's still, somewhere deep on the inside of me, the way I feel. I guess I don't feel really whole except when I'm with HIM. So when he's not there, I'm just a shell, kind of. He's like the spark and I'm the candle. And if the candle isn't lit, it can't give off radiance. Do I know what I'm talking about? Yes! But there's no way to really explain it.

September 30, Saturday

12:56 p.m.

I went to the mall with Jenny and Deanna after school Friday, and today we just hung out, then went to the ice rink. It was fun but not fun like it used to be. I want to be with Danny! They both know I've got a thing for him, and they tease me mercilessly, but in a way that's cool because it lets me know they think we're *something*.

I know Danny had to go to a regional football camp this weekend, and I really want him to be there learning to be the best of whatever he can be in every area of his life, but I still resent it in a way.

Good grief, girl, can you possibly be jealous? *Is it possible* to be jealous of a *thing*? I don't know! But for some reason I'm *really* fragmented about lots of my feelings these days.

I wish I had someone to talk to. Someone who

could *understand* where I'm at. Mom's looking at my life from her old-fashioned, overprotective side, and Jenny and Deanna would be looking at it from their dumb-as-I-am side. School counselor? No way, there are kids lining up in front of his door all the time. Shrink? Where would I get the money? Church person? . . . ummmm no. The things I call problems would probably make him laugh.

So . . . I guess I'm stuck with you, Daisy Diary. From now on you're going to be my alter ego, right? Well, what do you think?

You think I am jealous? Yikes! Maybe you're right and I *shouldn't* be jealous of him doing things he *ought* to do, should I? I thought . . . I don't know what I thought. Anyway I've got to always remember to respect *his* thoughts and concepts and needs, and remember that they may sometimes be different from mine. That's mature! And in the last analysis, what I really want, and will ever want, is what he wants and what is best for him!

I'm so glad Mom took psychology classes, and that she's shared some of the really good concepts with me. I'm going to take psychology classes too as soon as I'm old enough.

October 1, Sunday

2:27 a.m.

I guess it's really still Saturday! He'll be home to-day. I wonder if he'll call me. I hope he does. I really, really, really hope he does! He's got to! I'll die if he doesn't.

Ode to Danny

I miss your smile
I miss your touch
I miss you very, very much.
I hope, I hope that you miss me.
I'd miss you through eternity.

11:31 a.m.

Oh bleeding, bleeding, bleeding, wounded, hurting heart, how can you bear the pain? I'm too hurt to cry; still I'm crying inside so hard, I fear I am lit-erally drowning myself in my black, bitter acid tears.

Maybe Meg was lying. I hope she was! I know she was!!!! She COULD NOT have seen Danny rid-ing around last night with Tanya, please not Tanya.

She's such an overt slut—everyone knows it.

"Overt: done openly, without attempt at concealment." Why does my mind drift to stupid things like Mom giving me a dollar for every new word I start using. I'll *never* use that word again, ever! *Ever*! I wish I could tear it out of my mind.

Oh Danny, Danny, Danny, how could you do this to me? You promised me a room full of dandelions soon and a room full of red roses later.

I can understand how you might have found Mardie prettier than I am, or Molly more personable, or Jenny more everything! But Danny, how . . . how . . . why . . . why Tanya?

2:22 p.m.

I've been throwing up, with a headache and stuff. Mom thinks I've got the flu. I think I'll go take some of her Niteall. Sleep is the only escape I can think of. I wish I could sleep forever!

4:30 p.m.

Mom woke me about an hour ago. She had a hard time rousing me. When she finally did and told me Danny was on the phone, I tried to burrow down into my covers like a ground squirrel. Thank everything wonderful she insisted I take his call, and, with a shaking voice, I said, "Hello." I was feeling so scared and betrayed and lonely and lost, it was like a Stephen King movie, totally, totally unreal.

Danny said he'd missed me, and my first inclination was to scream at him that I knew about Tanya, so he couldn't have missed me *too much* ... but I couldn't. He sounded so sincere and happy that I didn't have the heart to rain on his parade. His words tumbled out in a jumble about how hard the team had worked, and how much they'd learned, and how fun it had been, and how when he got home late yesterday afternoon, he'd been so beat both physically and mentally that he'd gone straight to bed.

I'm sooo, sooo, sooooo relieved! I know Meg must have seen someone who just looked like him from a distance. She'd said it was "last night," and it's easy to *not* see things clearly in dim light.

Isn't it strange how your life can change from black tarry quicksand depression to bird-singing, lilac-blooming, sunshine happiness? That's what mine is now—well ... a little late for lilacs, but I find myself smiling, grinning, beaming all over (even on the inside of me). It's never too late for dandelions in one's life! Something deep in the deepest part of my heart tells me that *he* will *bring me one* when he comes by. Mom's going to her friend Nell's in a little while, so that won't be any problem, and Mrs. Brushel, "pokey nose," won't be able to see Danny and me drive away because her apartment faces on the side street, and ours is on the front.

> *Oh glorious day*
> *Hey, hey, hey*

I want to write a song to share all the happy music I feel inside with the world.

If I didn't have YOU, dear Daisy Diary, to share my happiness with, I positively, absolutely, think I would burst and splatter all over the room in little blobs of happy sunshine. Nutty, yeah?

"Yeah."

Okay, so now you're talking back!

Well, it's still the way it is, so there!

What will I wear?
How will I fix my hair?
No time to spare.

10:47 p.m.

I told Mom I was going to Jenny's to study. Then I alerted Jenny, and I went out with Danny.

Mom was really mad when I came in because I was supposed to be home by 9:30, but even her being cyber-spaced can't dampen my happiness! Oh, Daisy, Danny is so *wonderful*, so *perfect*, so *beautiful* . . . I know we shouldn't call males beautiful, BUT HE IS! He's like a young Greek god, a youthful David that Michelangelo sculpted. I'm so lucky, lucky, lucky to have HIM *like* ordinary me!

We played tennis; then we drove up to the top of Hampton Hill. I'd never been there before, but of course, I've heard about IT and actually once wondered if I'd ever be asked to go there.

The city down below us looked like a little fairyland of tinkling lights or a million-zillion miniature Christmas trees with blinking bulbs going on and off. Danny said he felt like we were in Alice's Wonderland or in Gulliver's travels.

He had promised me on the way up that he wasn't going to the place the kids call HOME BASE. You know the place where ... anyway, he said he just wanted to show me the lights and pretend we were Gulliver's travelers ourselves or on our own Aladdin-like magic carpet floating out over the world. He also said *not everyone* went up Hampton Hill to "do the deed," that a lot of them, like him, just went up to enjoy the view and the peace and outdoor wildness of everything. When he explained *that*, I felt so proud *of him* and so respected and safe *with* him that *I* covered *his* face with kisses. Actually it was the first time *I'd really* kissed a boy. Oh, little smacks with Jay and a couple of others, but never, never, never a real tight-type gooey kiss.

I'd never imagined the static electricity and mind-body control... maybe... *mind-out-of-control-power* of ... but anyway, just as I was beginning to float out into some kind of foreign, exotic never-never land, we saw a police car coming up the road toward us. I was so scared, I started sniveling.

Danny gave me a shake that made my teeth rattle. "Stop crying! Pull yourself together!" he said *very* sternly (actually, I guess it was just authoritatively, so I would stop blubbering). "You want to make the cops think I was trying to rape you or some other dumb thing?"

I blew my nose, wiped away the tears, and he apologized gently. "You know I wouldn't get you, above all people, into trouble for anything in the world."

The police shined their lights into our car, but by then we were sitting far apart and had turned the radio station to a hard rock one instead of romantic soft stuff. I was shaking so hard, I thought I was going to bounce out of the car.

"You kids better get out of here," they warned on their loudspeaker and Danny immediately obeyed.

On the way down the hill, Danny asked quietly, "You're a virgin, aren't you?"

I nodded ever so slightly, in some stupid way feeling almost embarrassed.

He pulled his arm from around my shoulder and sat up straight and stiff. "So am I."

Oh, Daisy, you don't know how safe that made me feel. I couldn't say this even to Jenny but . . . well, we didn't do *too much* beyond kiss, really soulful kissing and . . . but I'm really glad he's so respectful of both himself and me. He just gave me a little peck when we got home.

October 2, Monday

4:31 p.m.

Saw Danny in the hall outside the cafeteria. He said he had to eat with a couple of guys on the team because they were planning game strategies. It really hurt me because he seemed so distant, but I guess that's because he feels so responsible to the team. Actually, if I was a mature person, I would

---

27

probably feel proud of him because he takes his responsibilities so seriously . . . and actually I do! I DO! I DO! I've got to help him in every way to be the best *him* he can be! I can't wait till I can take some psych classes. Maybe I'll go to the library and get a book.

October 3, Tuesday

9:47 p.m.

Jenny and I went to the Pro Shop after school to get me some new soccer shorts, and then later I went to the market with Mom to get stuff for the party she's having Thursday night for her school's Honor Students. She's in charge of the program, and I'm proud of her. She's trying to train me to be one of her Honor Students when I'm in high school, and I'm trying. They do lots of fun things, like go to State and stuff, some even make it to Nationals. I don't know if I can do that, but I'm certainly going to give it my best try.

Mom took me out to dinner at Mi Casita, my very favorite Mexican restaurant, but somehow even that wasn't as fun as usual. I guess I'm really hung up on Danny. I don't seem to be able to really enjoy things when he's not there. I'm thinking about him, feeling him close to me, all the time. Even when I should be thinking about or doing other things. It's kind of like he's one of those songs that go around and around in your head, and you can't get it out. He seems to be always, always, always there. It's dumb!

Sorry, gotta go now and do homework. I'm not usually a procrastinator, but it's been hard to get settled down with it tonight.

October 5, Thursday

9:19 p.m.

I'm really getting miffed with Danny's team and his dad. Between the two of them, he's almost ignoring me. I know I should be more understanding and all that, and *I do* understand that his dad is renovating the big main dining room and needs *him*, and that *he's* very important to the team too, but there should be a few minutes for *ME* somewhere in the day or night. He tells me there will be soon. I hope I can wait. I guess I don't have any choice . . . wish I did.

October 7, Saturday

10:10 p.m.

Took Peg's place on the older tennis team at the very last moment at the State run-off. It was weird because I'd played all day with my own group, still . . . guess what? Can you believe we won! Me playing the best game I've ever played. It was a fluke because I've never done very well in doubles. It was awesome! Really truly awesome!

10:38 p.m.

It would have been *more* awesome if Danny had been there.

October 10, Tuesday

4:16 p.m.

Danny and I had lunch together and my heart was singing till Tad came up and dragged him off for a guy thing. I am beginning to feel *deeply* resentful ... jealous? *Yes! Jealous* of everything and everybody, especially Tanya, who always seems to be hanging around. I hate her! And I hate Tad and the other guys who are always kissing up to him because Danny has the cool car and he's older and ... I'M GREEN-EYED, SUSPICIOUS, ENVIOUS, STUPID and I've got to stop it!

I WILL!

I HAVE! *I have! I have!*

I am now again the noble, mature person I've always been, and I don't kiss up to Danny because of all the above things. It's just because ...

because ...

he's so LOVEABLE! AND I LOVE HIM! I really, truly honestly do and I'm sooooooo glad I've got you to share both my joy and sorrow with. Jenny and Deanna are my very best friends, but I don't think they'd understand like you do. I know they wouldn't ... couldn't.

Thank you, thank you, thank you, very best dear friend Diary. You're like the very deepest innermost part of me that understands all my trials and sorrows and weaknesses and insecurities and ugly stupidities ... and you *still* tolerate me, think kindly of me and ... sometimes even love and respect me. What would I ever, ever do without you? You are my psychiatrist, my mentor, my cheerleader, my advisor ... sort of a silent advisor, but you are important in my life. I can cough up the gruesomest, most revolting, nauseous things in the world, and you never lecture or preach; you just accept me exactly as I am. I wish more people could do that. Maybe Danny isn't as busy as he says;

maybe he's just trying to dump me easy, do you think? Please tell me you don't think that.

October 11, Wednesday

2:31 a.m.

I'm such a duh, dumb, gullible dweeb sometimes, like now. I can't think of one single positive in my life. I know that's stupid and ridiculous but sometimes I'M stupid and ridiculous—like now! Everything good and sunshiney and joyous in life has disintegrated before my eyes. I feel lonely, lost, alone, helpless, and hopeless. . . . It's black and spiderwebby, sticky and scary in here. Help, help, help! Somebody get me out!

October 12, Thursday

5:12 a.m.

I must have cried myself to sleep because my pillow is still wet, but that seems to have drained away all the cold, evil blackness because out my window I can see the pinkness in the east turning to yellow, so la-la-la—the sun will come out "to-morrow," which is really today, right?

October 13, Friday

4:37 p.m.

I've only got a minute because Danny passed me in the hall and asked me to go to a party with him tonight. Sorry, I gotta go. What am I saying? I'm *not* sorry, I'm *elated*!

12:21 p.m.

Daisy:
   Everyone was there. Lots of jocks and cheerleaders from *high* school, plus some older guys. It was stupendous! Danny was treated like a Knight on the Hill or something. And they treated *ME* like I was someone too! Can you believe it, me? A princess at a party?
   Kelly's parents had gone away for the weekend, so the guys brought in a whole keg of beer, and at first I said I didn't drink. Danny gave me a dirty look like I was embarrassing him and started flirting with Marcie, the prettiest girl there, and I felt I *had* to. After a while I was as happy and silly as everybody else, and I didn't know I could have so much fun.

We were in Kelly's basement playroom, and the music was so loud, it practically vibrated the walls. Kids were screaming and bouncing on the couches or just snuggled up in couples around in corners. Danny and I were slow-dancing to the sounds that reverberated through our bodies like the big bass drums in the Fourth of July parade. It felt good. We were part of it. It was like something new and wonderful and different.

Then suddenly we seemed to be all alone, just the two of us in the whole universe dancing together as one, part of the music, the flashing colors, the differentness.

Oh, Daisy, it was so wonderful and warm. I belonged. I really truly honestly belonged. For the first time in my life, I was on top of the heap where *everybody wants to be*! and usually doesn't make it, and it was grand, grand, GRAND!

The only problem is . . . well, I guess I can tell you; actually, I've got to tell you, or I'll burst. Well, on the way home Danny pulled off the road by the old haunted house and insisted we . . . you know. I was scared and . . . he was drunk and rough, and I really had to scream and fight him off. . . . I promised myself I wouldn't EVER again think about that part of the night! I'd blot it out of my mind completely because I know it was just because Danny was drunk. Anyway, I fought and hit back on and on as he hissed at me every bad word I've ever heard, but at last he finally gave up, and calling me a "boob, Mama's baby," he took me home and almost pushed me out of the car.

But I'm NOT GOING TO THINK ABOUT THAT.

I HOPE HE WON'T REMEMBER IT EITHER WHEN HE SOBERS UP. IT WASN'T THE *REAL* DANNY. IT WAS *THE ALCOHOL* AND I THINK HE MIGHT HAVE HAD A FEW PUFFS ON A . . . but that's all over. Tomorrow we'll both apologize to each other and do some serious talking about where we're going to go from here.

It's going to be alright! It's *got to be* alright! He'll probably call me as soon as he wakes up.

I HOPE!

    I HOPE!

        but . . .

Some little, scary, writhing creature inside me is . . . asking . . . did he mean to hit me? . . . Did he mean to say all the terrible, evil, awful things he said to me? . . . Did he expect me to . . . do it . . . for the first time in my whole life, when he was acting like someone I didn't even know? I am sooo confused. How could my precious, sweet, tender Danny change to . . . him? It must have been the alcohol or maybe someone put PCP in his . . . I don't know. I don't want to know! In fact, I never want to think about it again! IT DID NOT HAPPEN!

"But it did!"

Stay out of this, Daisy. NO! Help me. Please *help me* sort this out. Did Danny mean it when he said, "Everyone was doing it," and how long did I expect to "just lead him on and tease him" and all the other vulgar, crude things?

I hate to admit this, even to you, but some little part of me is wondering if he really is a virgin, or if that too was a line, just another part of *his* planned persuasion technique.

NO! NO! NO! HE WAS JUST DRUNK AND STONED, AND HE WON'T REMEMBER A THING. PLEASE, PLEASE LET IT BE THAT WAY!

October 14, Saturday

11:30 a.m.

Danny hasn't called. I wonder if I should call him? No, he's just sleeping late.

And I could be in deep trouble. Mom thought I went out with Jenny and Deanna last night. I told her Mrs. Tanner had car trouble on the way home. I hope she doesn't find out I lied. I hate to lie to her; it always brings in so many dumb complications.

1:16 p.m.

Danny *still* hasn't called. I'm getting a little worried.

2:10 p.m.

I'm *a lot* worried!

3:02 p.m.

I'm sure Danny's dad woke him up and made him go straight to work. Oh I do, do, do, do hope that's it.

4:12 p.m.

I called the restaurant and asked them to have Danny return my call as soon as possible. I told them it was very important.

10:56 p.m.

Danny hasn't returned my call. Maybe he didn't get my message. Could it possible be that he doesn't want to talk to me? Maybe it's something macho about him wanting *me* to apologize first. I *can do that*! Gladly, happily, and I will, first thing on Monday. I'll track him down after his first class. But . . . what if? There *will not* be a what if! I must be positive!

October 15, Sunday

10:56 p.m.

I've waited by the phone all day, didn't go out of the house once. Mom invited me to go with her to the grand opening of a new Boutique Center, but I said I had an upset stomach. It wasn't really a lie because I have an upset-all-over.

I wonder what possibly could have happened to Danny. Is he mad at me? So mad that he'll never speak to me again through all of forever, or just waiting long enough to let me suffer and come to my senses? What does that mean?

October 16, Monday

2:57 a.m.

I don't think I'll ever be able to sleep again. Dorky me. I'm so mixed up. Does Danny really want me to . . . expect me to? . . . Oh, how I wish *you* could talk back. *You're* the only one I can talk to, and you lie there like you *don't care*, aren't even concerned that my heart is breaking and my life is in an absolute mess.

Mom told me when I got my first diary on my tenth birthday that it would help me sort out my thoughts, that by writing things down and then re-reading them, I would make better decisions in my life, be more realistic instead of unrealistic. . . . Now I'm facing the biggest decision in my life, and what are you doing to help me? Nothing! I don't think I'll ever rely upon you again; you're nothing but a stupid, dumb book filled with little baby scribblings. I guess I've grown beyond you.

5:02 p.m.

I can't believe a body and a mind and a soul could hurt as much as mine. I feel like I've been smashed and bashed and run over and squashed by a steamroller and bulldozer and wrecking ball. Every atom of my body is bleeding. Oh pain, pain, pain go away.

I wish Mom was here, so I could curl up on her lap and have her hug me so tight, I'd feel little and safe and secure and loved. . . . and I could just blubber out all my pains, and she could kiss them away and make them better like she used to do; but I guess I'm too big for that now. I've got problems that I have to solve for myself. Being *sort of grown up* isn't nearly as much fun as I thought it would be!!!!!!

I'm so very, very, very glad I have *YOU*, dear Daisy Diary; I know I said last night I wasn't, but

I am! I need you now more than I ever have. I'd feel like a silly jackass talking to Jenny or Deanna or Molly or . . . And, of course, having lied to Mom, I've cut off that route.

Anyway, Danny's words are still pounding in my ears and on my heart. Oh, they are so hurting and humiliating, I can hardly tell them to you . . . but I have to. Their loudness is growing in my ears till I can't stand it; I really, really can't! This morning I was standing outside Danny's first period class when the bell rang, and as the kids shoved out I pushed up close to him and whispered, "Danny, we've got to talk. I'm sooooo sorry about Saturday night. . . ."

He . . . I can not write it. . . . pushed me aside like I was garbage. I caught up with him. "Please Danny, I don't want to break up—I . . ."

He sneered down at me. "Maybe someday, little girl, when I'm going to a Sunday School picnic . . ." His buddies were around, and they all started laughing. I could feel the blood rushing up into my face and my ears ringing, but I couldn't move. I was like a dazed animal hypnotized by the lights of an oncoming car.

Everybody in the hall was laughing at me then. It was like a slow-motion horror-psychotic picture show.

At last my imprisoned body became mobile and ran down the endlessly long, dark hall tunnel with laughing, poking, making-fun grotesque figures on every side. The whole school—principal, teachers and all—was making fun of me. I must have gone crazy for a time because it really did seem like that was what was happening. I wonder if that's possible? I mean for someone to go absolutely, totally crazy insane for a few minutes? Anyway, next thing I knew, I found myself on the bus, I hoped, going home.

I'm so scared now, I don't know what to do. Am I going to have crazy fits from now on for the rest of my life every time something traumatic happens to me? Please tell me I'm not. Please, please tell me that!

"Okay, you're not."

You told me! You really did tell me! You can't imagine how much better that makes me feel!

"I'm glad."

Now you've got to help me decide what I'm going to do next.

"Oops, sorry, I can't do that."

You've got to!

"Well . . ."

I guess it amounts to . . . if I want to keep Danny, then . . .

"Then what?"

Danny's right; I'm just being a little girl, booby baby boob tube.

"I don't think so."

Ha . . . you *can't* think! You're just paper.

"Am I? Or am I your conscience?"

Well, if you *are*, butt out! I want to make this decision by myself.

"Without common sense, reasoning, consideration of 'cause and effect,' like we learned in science, or 'actions vs. consequences,' like we learned in mental health?"

You're sounding like Mom.

"So?"

So, I'm fourteen years old. I *don't want* to sound like my mother.

"I know, but . . ."

No buts! I'm going to do this *my* way. Without Danny I'm a totally useless nothing, a *nothing* going nowhere.

October 20, Friday

4:37 p.m.

It has been four long, endlessly, snail-crawling, slow-motioned, stupid, ugly, useless days. I can't think in my classes; I want to scream at my teachers; I won't talk to Mom—in fact, she's kissing up to me trying to find out what's wrong, until sometimes I feel like I want to turn on her like a cat with its claws out. I'm even beginning to think maybe I'll burn *you* and pretend none of the past month's gibberish shit ever happened. I don't usually swear, but that's exactly what it's been! Never has a word been more correctly used! Danny is trying (AND SUCCEEDING) to stay away from me like I have the plague, even though I've almost stalked him night and day, at least in my mind.

Everybody's ignoring me! Well not everybody; Jenny and Deanna and my *real* friends all just keep telling me Danny's not worth the pain I'm feeling. They want me to flush him and sometimes I think

I should. I WANT TO! But I *can't*!!!! I wish like everything I could, or . . . MAYBE I CAN!

10:58 p.m.

I'm trying, I really am . . . but I still can't! It's like he's a part of me, an arm or a leg, or both my arms and legs put together; I don't think anyone else in the world could understand that, especially not Mom. She and Dad fought from as long back as I can remember. Not big, screaming, hitting fights but quiet, polite little "cut-down" blows. That's probably what makes me so insecure and all the other negative things I am. But *that's not true*. All my friends feel the same way: not as good as, not as pretty as, not as smart as, not as personable as, not as tall as, not as thin as, etc. we want to be. We're all anxiety-ridden, unconfident, scared, unstable, wavering nutcases trying to carve out our own little niche and not doing too well most times.

"I didn't know you felt that way about Dad and Mom."

Uhhh . . . I don't really. In fact everything seemed to be very story-bookish until Dad lost his job and . . .

"His self-confidence?"

Yeah, and he started just sitting around the house or taking on-the-road selling-stuff jobs.

"And staying away longer and longer."

I don't want to think about those times, nor Mom or Dad's troubles! I just wish *she'd* been more "there for him!" *Go away!* I've got my own problems now! And Danny *isn't* one of them! It's all going to work out! It has to! He just has to learn *he cannot* handle liquor.

"What if he doesn't?"

I'll die. I'll just shrivel up and die! I'm beginning to do it already. I can feel it. I actually sense, deeper than feelings, that my atoms and cells and DNA and all the other stuff that makes me alive are slowly ceasing to exist.

"I've heard you say stupid things before, but that's about the stupidest."

Which proves to me that even *you* don't understand. AND I'm not talking to *you* anymore. I'm going to be talking only to myself from now on. I don't need your negativity or belittling of me! I'm going to think only of what Danny wants *us* to do. When we broke up, I was acting like a scared little mama's brat, and besides, *"everyone is doing it."*

"*Everyone is not* doing it!"

Everyone that I want to be like *is*. I felt, at last, that I belonged and was princess to his being prince, at his friend's party.

"Are you sure about this?"

I'm sure I'm sure! I *want* to belong! I *want* to be tight! I *want* to be a *twosome* with Danny! A *somebody*, not a *onesome nobody*! Besides, in movies and books and magazines and TV, even on cornflakes boxes, sex is the *epitome*, the beginning and the end of all things, fun and good and rapturous. It's supposed to be like being carried away into another world of joy, pleasure, love, and ecstasy.

"What about the vow of chastity you made at your youth conference last summer?"

Butt out! *Butt out! Butt out*! This is between me

and Danny AND *YOU'RE* NOT A PART OF US
ANYMORE!

October 26, Thursday

10:47 p.m.

Six, endless, boring, gray, stupid days have passed,
each one getting longer and more useless and
empty than the rest. Last night I went to a party at
Kathy's, but it was all girls and seemed like a kindergarten gathering.

Kathy's mom showed pictures of some of the
kids as they were growing up. That was the bore
of all bores because it was long before I moved
here.

I feel like a complete zombie. Life has lost its
color and flavor and music. I want Danny back so
much, I'm obsessed by it. When I see him in the
halls, he ignores me like I'm invisible. I saw Pam
Doms in his car one day and wanted to literally
beat up on her. I could feel myself tearing out her
hair. I'm so ashamed; I've never felt that way before. It's scary and hurtful, very, very hurtful!

Actually I'm beginning to feel trapped and suffocated in this gray, nothing, empty existence. I
want out! I need lights, music, excitement. What
can I do? He won't talk to me, and I can't leave the
kind of message I want to leave on his voice mail

for fear his dad or someone else will hear it. Sometimes I wish I could go back to being a little kid again with none of these torturous problems eating away at me like flesh- and guts- and eye-eating piranha fish.

I want to feel like I felt the night I was with Danny at Kelly's party. Happy and excited and important! I've *got* to get him back. But how?

I've tried talking to him.

I've tried telephoning him.

I've tried praying it would happen.

I'm tempted to go to a bookstore and get a magic book that tells how to cast spells. *THAT* should let you know how totally, totally, totally desperate I am.

Maybe I could make a videotape showing him, telling him how *totally* I am tied to him. How I respect his decisions and desires, and that I am willing to do every little thing in the world the way he wants it. Maybe I could even . . . NO, *that's* ridiculous! *I read somewhere once* that "Love is a form of insanity." It was supposed to be funny, but could that possibly be true?

Maybe I'll just stick a note through the little slot in his locker. What have I got to lose at this point?

"Your dignity?"

Get out of my face . . . rather, my head!

"Your self-respect?"

SHUT UP! It's about time I started living my own life, without *you* and Mom always telling me when to breathe in and when to breathe out. *I'm going to do it* and I'M going to write it *right now*! So try to blow that out of your paper nose!

5:57 p.m.

Dear Daisy:

I'm soooo, sooooo sorry about last night. I guess I'm rude and mean to you because you . . . you're *you*! I'm more mad at myself than I am at you. You know that don't you? And I NEED YOU! You're better than *anyone* on the Internet by about a billion-zillion-kat-tillion times.

And I'm soooooooooooooooo!!!!!!!!!!!!! scared! I left a dumb, stupid, groveling, tear-soaked note in Danny's locker, and now I'm mortified. I don't think I'll ever be able to show my face at school again. Oh why, why, why didn't I listen to you? I can just see him showing off the idiotic note to all the guys on the team and them laughing at me, the dumbest dunce of all time.

I shouldn't ever have told him that the *only thing* I wanted in *my* life was for him to be my Pygmalion. Remember the Greek sculptor who carved the statue that he fell in love with, and it became real? The movie *My Fair Lady* was made about it, only this time I want it to be Danny who makes me, an ignorant girl, into the grand and important person that he wants me to be.

We studied about Pygmalion in English, and it

seemed so sensitive and beautiful. *Now* as I think it over, it seems just stupid and dumber than dumb!

How could I have ever done it? How could *you* let me do it? But then HOW COULD YOU OR ANYONE HAVE STOPPED ME?

6:03 p.m.

I wonder if Mom could change me to another school. I don't care how long I'd have to be on the bus or in what kind of a horrible area it might be.

9:31 p.m.

Be still my singing heart for just a sec while I tell my beloved Daisy the wondrous news: DANNY CALLED! And he isn't mad or disgusted at me or anything. He said he thought I was mad and disgusted with him, and that he was even more mad and disgusted with himself . . . and sooooo sorry. . . . He certainly didn't act that way in the hall . . . but maybe he was just embarrassed then because . . . well, because we'd both been so . . . you know. *I hope you know* because I'm sure I don't! Anyway, the past is all over, and he wants to forget it, pretend it never happened, erase it, which we have! And we're going to start all over as though we're just meeting again, *except* the dandelions! I insisted that we keep the rooms full of dandelions and roses in our forevers. He called me his "Earth Angel" and said he "needs me" more than I'll ever know. Isn't that beautiful?

He's coming over tomorrow night at 8:30, and everything will work out exactly like in my dreams. Mom is going to see her friend Melba in Concord, so she'll be home really late and—

Oh, Daisy, I'm so filled with love and joy and laughter, I feel like . . . like a dandelion that has reached its full ethereal potential and is ready to explode its lovely little softies into all the universe.

I'd better go to sleep now, so I'll be rested and as attractive as it's possible for me to be for tomorrow. Maybe Mom will let me have my hair trimmed and if I'm superduper lucky, get that ever-so-cool outfit I saw at the mall. It's kind of expensive, so I think not. But who knows since this seems to be the luckiest of all my lucky days?

October 28, Saturday

8:26 p.m.

Oh, Daisy, I can't believe it—Danny just called and said they're having a big banquet at the restaurant, and two of the waiters have called in sick. He's really upset with his dad for making him work, but he's stuck. I tried to make him feel better about it, but all the time I was crying on the inside of myself. I've spent the whole live-long day trying to get ready for tonight and now . . . blah . . .

Jenny invited me to go to Hot Springs with her family and spend the day, but I turned that down; now there's just boring you and me.

It would have been fun to go the Springs with Mr. and Mrs. Jordan. They're the kind of family everybody wants! A cool mom, a funny dad, two little boys, and a "Jerky Jenny." That's what Todd and Terry call her when they're mad at her. Anyway, I guess she's my very best friend. She was the first person I met when we moved here. I didn't know up from down at the school till she came by and saved me. I'll always be appreciative of that. I guess I'm really fortunate to have friends like Jenny and Deanna and Molly and Meg. We're a bunch of tomboy-girl dorks, and basically we don't get in trouble.

All of us, except Meg, went to the Methodist Christian three-day Youth Conference both this year and last, and we're all dedicated to being ethical and God-fearing and kind and honest, and all the other things we were taught as we swam and hiked and sang and built tepees, and all the other stuff that is supposed to make us well-rounded, caring-for-our-fellow-man-and-woman types of people. Meg's dad wouldn't let her go because they're Catholics, but my mom and Deanna's folks let *us* go even though we're *not* Methodists. My mom says goodness and truth are goodness and truth no matter where we find them.

Wouldn't it be positively heavenly if I could get Danny to go with us to the youth conference next summer? There's no "messing around" up there, but it would be a good chance to learn everything about each other from the inside out.

Jenny met Doug there last year and they're still writing letters and communicating on the Net as often as they can, which isn't often because he doesn't have a computer at home.

Well, at least daydreaming in writing has made me feel better. I'll just continue to think about Danny and me at the youth conference together in the open piney woods by the lake and the two creeks. It would be sooo positively wonderful. Maybe he could be a junior counselor because he's older. I love daydreaming!

I think I'm going to make some chocolate chip cookies, turn on my kind of music, cuddle up, and just let my mind wander.

'Night, sweet dreams, Daisy.

I love you! I hope you can still love me!!!!!!!!!!!!!!!!!!!!!!!!!

October 29, Sunday

2:30 a.m.

I woke up wondering how it's going to be with me and Danny. He's such a wonderful, sweet person when he's not drinking and using. I hope he never does that again. Maybe it will be my job to keep him straight and sober and virtuous. I feel that's what he wants to be, as I know it's really what I want to be. Maybe it's my calling to help him be strong and resist all the negatives in life, so he can make *the very best and most of himself!* I know he can do anything and be anything he wants, particularly if I'm by his side and helping him!

I'm sooooooooooo grateful for my mom, who has always taught me to strive for good and right things. Now maybe I'm going to have the opportunity to help Danny with those things. I am soooooooooo happy, I'm just bubbling and purring inside. Now I know how a kitty feels in front of a fireplace or on someone's lap.

11:21 a.m.

Danny called. His dad's letting him take off the afternoon and he "wants to be with me if I want to be with him." Do birds want to fly? Do fish want to swim? I gotta go do my hair and my nails and decide what to wear and try to magically cover up the rotten *volcanolike zit* that's popped up on my face. Why now? Why, why NOW!

I wonder if boys are as embarrassed by zits as girls are? I don't think so—they couldn't be.

Oh, dearest-friend-in-the-world Daisy, I'm so glad I have you! I want to talk to someone! I need to talk to someone! I've got to talk to someone!!!!! But I'm sooooooo embarrassed! So humiliated! So hurt! I mean hurt both physically and mentally—as well as *emotionally*! I don't think I'll ever recover. I don't see how I can. It's like a hideous nightmare, and I want to tell you about it, but it's so depraved. . . . I can't.

But I've *got* to unload. I feel like the horror of it all is building up inside me until I'm physically stretching out like a balloon and will soon pop into smithereens. I still can't believe it happened. Maybe it didn't. Maybe I've just gone crazy. Some weird little part of me wants to think *that. It* would be easier to handle than the truth.

"Tell *me*. It will make *you* feel better."

Oh Daisy, it was soooo terrible. Though not at first. Danny picked me up on the corner by Bigbee's and I sat way on my side in case any of the neighbors were around. He teased me about that, and we laughed like we'd done when we first met. I was goose bumpity—it seemed so wonderful. Then he told me he had to stop by his place to get something. I've forgotten what it was—I was so excited to see inside the old Pederson mansion.

We walked around the yard and the humongous old, old, old shady trees beckoned me to play hide-and-seek with them, but I resisted, and suggested Danny be not Prince Arthur but young, handsome, perfect *Prince Danny*. I would be his Guinevere. It was true fairytale stuff; the whole place, and time, and feeling.

After a while he took my hand, kissed it, and led me into the house. I almost swooned—it was so appropriate to our pretending. I could hear the heralds playing their horns for us while my heart galloped around inside of me like a white steed.

Danny took me into their study, which had a stone fireplace big enough to be a child's playhouse. The walls were covered with books, many in glass cases, and the big old, red, soft leather chairs and couch were giant sized. Danny sprawled out in a huge, huge Daddy Bear chair and I curtsied to him. He laughed, threw out his arms and yelled, "Dance for me, wench."

I wanted to explain to him what "wench" really meant, but that would have broken the mood, so I picked up a cloth that was over a little end table and gigglingly started swaying around.

After a minute or two his mood changed, and he ordered, "Take off your clothes."

I stopped, dumbfounded.

"Take off your clothes and dance dirty for me," he commanded.

I looked at him with unbelief. Before my eyes he had changed from Dr. Jekyll to Mr. Hyde.

In slow motion I watched him jump over the coffee table toward me. It was like HE was a *stranger*, and I wasn't *ME* anymore. I was just *a thing*. I started crying, and he called me vile names. When I tried to fight him off, he slapped me across the face. I couldn't believe what was happening, and I was so scared, I started screaming for help. He hit me *hard* then and put his hand over my mouth, calling me a bitch and a "ho" that was just trying to get him into trouble, but to forget it because no one was around.

Despite my tears and pleadings, he raped me vilely. It had nothing, nothing, nothing to do with LOVE. It was doglike, primeval ... everything that would forever remind me of rape and deception and debauchery. I staggered to my feet and fell against an end table. He grabbed the beautiful big lamp in time to save it, then hit me in the back with such force that I crumpled to the floor. And then he yelled at me to "get up and get out," that a baby like me needed to "get home to my mommy." He said I knew *why* I'd come there, that I was just a blank, blank, forever blank, blank tease and stuff.

I can't believe what happened next. I found myself kneeling at his feet telling him how sorry *I was* and sniveling on about my love for him. Thinking it would have been completely different if I hadn't led him on unknowingly—I tried to explain, but he pushed me away and said he needed and wanted someone who *really wanted* to, and *knew how to* love him. Then he half-dragged me to the door and shoved me out.

It was beginning to get dark, and I was scared because his house is halfway across town from ours, and I had no money.

By the time I'd stumbled down his path to the street, I'd convinced myself I'd have to go back, apologize, and get him to take me home. But at that moment his car roared out the driveway, down the street, and around the corner. I started shaking and realizing that the streets got meaner as they got darker. I started running.

It was thirty-one blocks from his house to ours. I know, because I counted every single one of them to keep my sanity.

About halfway home I heard a police car coming toward me with its siren on. My first instinct was to go into the street and flag it down so they'd safely take me home, then I realized that I obviously looked like I'd been raped, and they'd probably accuse Danny of it! *Then* Mom . . . and the whole world would know what had happened. I couldn't handle that. So I hid behind some bushes until the police car had passed.

As soon as I saw its lights disappear in the distance I started running again faster than ever. I had to go through a bad part of town and expected to see gangs of boisterous guys hangin' and looking for trouble on every corner, as well as prostitutes hawking their wares at each streetlamp, but it was really quiet, almost deadly quiet. It must have been too early or eating time or something because I'd seen pictures on the news of complete bedlam in that area.

Once a dog started chasing me, and I had an adrenaline rush that practically took me flying off the sidewalk. It must have been a big, old, fat, lazy dog though because he just chased me about a block, but by that time the blood was gushing so hard in my ears that I was about to pass out.

I wanted with everything in me to turn back and go sit on Danny's front porch steps till his dad or someone got home, but I figured that I must be more than halfway to our house. As they say, I was past "the point of no return."

Well, anyway, as you can see I finally made it

here and thank goodness Mom wasn't home because when I looked in the mirror I almost shocked myself silly. I don't know what she would have done. Perspiration had kinked my hair up into tight little knots and her mascara I had put on had run down my cheeks until I looked like I had two black eyes. They matched the big bruise on my face. My blouse was torn and one pocket was practically ripped out of my new linen pants.

Suddenly I became frantic! How would I ever explain to Mom? She'd probably call the police, and it would be headlines in the paper, and everybody in town would know, and I'd have to quit school from embarrassment, and Danny might be sent away to a juvenile hall somewhere, where *he'd* be viciously and sadistically abused by drug-crazed thugs. Maybe maimed or killed.

I quickly washed my face, got out of my telltale clothes, put on Mom's old robe, and hurried down to the carports. I remembered having seen an old can of grease behind the Knotts' parking space. Sneakily I walked past it, and dipping a stick in the gook, swiped it back and forth a couple of times on my clothes, then bundled them up and took them back into the house.

Spreading my pants and shirt out in the bathtub, I tried to make them look like I'd been hit by a car and knocked down in a grease puddle. The whole story sounded pretty good to me, but I wasn't sure Mom would buy it. I couldn't think though of any other way I could explain my bruised cheek and my swollen eye to her.

I then had to clean the grease out of the tub, which took forever. Every minute I became more and more scared that Mom would come in, and my story wouldn't fly. But thank goodness, by the time she did get home, I'd cleaned the tub, showered, washed my hair, and had my soiled clothes all piled on newspapers on the washer with a pathetic little note: "PLEASE, MOM DON'T EVER MAKE ME LOOK AT THESE THINGS AGAIN. IT WOULD BE LIKE RELIVING THE ACCIDENT."

Mom was cool. She came in and said immediately, "Baby, what happened to your face?"

I gulpingly explained about the make-believe accident (but the gulps were real)!

She held me in her arms and sobbed how glad she was that I wasn't hurt worse.

I begged her please to not report the accident, as I'd been jogging, and I was sure I was the one who kind of ran into the dusk-colored car in the dusk, and that I was almost positive the driver wasn't even aware that he/she had hit me, and also that I wasn't even sure which corner it was on because it had stunned me a little . . . no, a lot!

Mom hugged me even tighter as I begged her never to mention the foolish accident again and swore I'd be much more careful and aware in the future.

Mom promised.

I feel so dishonorable and dirty about lying to her, almost more despicable about that than about what actually happened at Danny's. I was partly responsible for *that* in a way, but *she* didn't do anything. . . . I'm such a bad, lying, finagling, hypocrite!!!!! Mom would probably be better off if I hadn't been born, or if I had died when I almost drowned in the pool when I was four, or ate the aspirin when I was three, or . . . but I *didn't*, and she's still burdened by me and probably will be the rest of her life. I'm sure *I'm the reason* she hasn't married again! Who would want to be saddled with me?

I think I better go to bed, I'm completely cycled. I don't know when I've ever been so twisted and drained in my whole life.

Maybe I'll be lucky and there won't be a tomorrow!

October 30, Monday

11:57 a.m.

Mom sat by my bed and scratched my back and sang me to sleep. As I finally drifted off, I remember I was slipping back into my no-cares childhood: dolls, tricycles, little red-and-blue plastic swimming pool on the front lawn. Now it's reality time again, and it's unbearable, positively, absolutely, without question unbearable.

11:46 p.m.

I've slept practically the whole day.

10:06 p.m.

I can hear Mom getting ready for bed in her room, and I'm glad. I can't stand to talk with her any-more. She's trying to be *so* loving and helpful and I'm being so . . . what is a word for someone as de-ceitful and fake as I am? Maybe there isn't one. Anyway, I'm glad for sleep. It's the only way I can escape, not have to face it, not have to decide what to do, not have to pretend and lie. I'm trying to blot out the whole Danny thing and not think about it, trying to deceive myself into believing that it's all a disgusting dream that didn't ever really hap-pen.

Mom's really worried about me. She thinks I'm in shock or something, or that I had a little brain concussion or . . . who knows?. . . . who cares?

November 2, Thursday

1:14 a.m.

I just woke up from a really weird, strange, science fiction-type dream. I know *I'm losing it* and I've got to *get myself together*! This ESCAPE THING can't go on the rest of my life. Sometime, someplace, I've got to face reality and I guess it might as well be here and *NOW*!

1:41 a.m.

I'm sitting at my window looking at a smiling quarter moon, a sky sprinkled with shining, twinkling stars, and listening to the music of the night and smelling its fragrances. God made a beautiful, wonderful world . . . and I'm just a zit on it! No I'm not! He loves me!

This is really funny; I just sang a sweet song that I didn't even know I knew—it was tucked so far back in my little girlhood. The song just sort of came out from nowhere, and I sang it to the moon and stars and all the nice night things.

> *"Jesus loves me this I know*
> *For the Bible tells me so."*

I think the song has many verses about kind, loving, helping, forgiving things, like:

> "He will teach me right from wrong.
> I am weak but HE is strong."

I feel so much better. I'm glad I thought of the song. It is going to help me get my jigsawed life back together again. Ummm, I feel so content, I think I'll yawn and stretch and take another little nap. I'll get things straightened out when it's morning.

5:22 a.m.

The sun is beginning to peek out over the eastern horizon. A whole flock of birds must have come in during the night, and they are all singing their little hearts out. Someone once said, "Life is good, and we must be *good to it*." Okay, today is the day I start! But where? First with the *Danny thing*. I'm still crushed and broken and splattered emotionally, and I've thought about nothing but having Mom change me to another school, but I can't think of one earthly reason why I *can* ask her to, *except Danny*, and I can't mention that to her. I NEVER, NEVER WILL! And I hate to say this even to you dear Daisy . . . but . . . I do *still love* him. I love him with every particle of my being. He can be soooo gentle, so caring, so humorous and playful, yet so formally mannered when necessary. He says awesome things to me that make me feel like a goddess or truly an "Earth Angel." *Everybody* at school *loves* him. Absolutely everybody! Teachers, coaches, kids, janitors, and cafeteria ladies. Especially the cafeteria ladies! He's so funny and flattering and respectful to them. Mrs. Schmidts even brought him some chocolate chip cookies she'd made at home. He said HE *NEEDS ME* to become the brilliant lawyer he wants to become, or anything else successful.

I think about the rooms full of dandelions and roses he will someday give me, and his wonderful, gentle sensitiveness, and the wonderful way he smells, and his strong arm around my shoulder. You can never even guess the protection and belonging feelings that gives me and the sense of joy and love and *self-worth*. I'm *someone* when I'm with him! And I want him back so much that every cell in my body aches. Never have I been happier than when I was with him, never more fulfilled, more at peace, more at ease. Actually, I'm not really sure I *can* live without him, nor if I want to. Ugg, that was a nasty breeze that whipped through my mind. There's no way I would do that!

And, I've never even tried to look at *the* incident from *his* point of view. I know ever since his family moved here, he's been working more hours a day for his dad than any kid should ever have to work, *and* he's been quarterback of the football team, and on some school council, and who knows what else. Also, since they've been redoing the banquet room and some of the other rooms one by one at the restaurant, his dad hasn't given him any time off at all. I *know* he hasn't because if he had, he would have been with me. He hasn't even had time to return my calls. I'm not sure when he has time to sleep, or if he does.

Once in a mental health class, we learned that sleep deprivation can make people do all sorts of weird things . . . like hallucinate and lose their sense of depth perception and not think clearly . . . I wonder . . . could Danny's crazed behavior be attributed to overwork and sleep deprivation? I think it very well could be, and he's probably so humiliated and stunned by what he did to me that he is in even worse shape than I am. No wonder he hasn't called. I can just imagine how he's beating up on himself. But he *wasn't* himself then! Oh, I've got to talk to him! Do you think I should? Would it make things worse? It couldn't!

I can just see him suffering and not knowing how to get himself out of the mess. I've got to help him, I really have! I'm probably the only one who can because I was the one who . . . made him—*caused* him to get out of control. He said I did! He said *I* did loud and clear!

UMMMMMMM, now it's just a matter of deciding how I should go about doing whatever . . .

6:22 a.m.

I know how I'm going to do it. I'm just going to write him a note telling him the simple, honest truth; "Dear Danny: There is no way I can live without you. I'm so, so, so, so sorry for everything! I *cannot* live without you. Annie."

I'll stick it through the slot in his locker. I'll do it first thing tomorrow morning.

4:37 p.m.

I didn't see Danny at school at all today. I'm worried and confused. I hope I didn't make a totally total fool and laughingstock of myself.

If some of the monstrous things happen that I'm thinking might, I'll never be able to show my face again. THAT WAS SUCH A STUPID, ASSININE, LEAVE-MYSELF-WIDE-OPEN-FOR-A-SECOND-TAKEDOWN THING TO DO!!!!!!! Why do I do things without thinking them out carefully first or talking to somebody about them? Talk about a no-brainer! But I *want* a boyfriend soooooooo much! I *want HIM* so much. Our times together were the best times in my whole life, or ever-will-be life. Now I've probably blown it completely! How stupid can a person get?

11:49 p.m.

Oh happy day! Danny called! He was crying and he begged my forgiveness over and over. He doesn't understand how he could have done such despicable things and says he hated himself to the point that he wanted to drive off a cliff or something. He about broke my heart, and he says he can't understand how I can be so forgiving. He doesn't *understand* either that I probably understand him even better than he does himself. I realize how hard he's been working both at school and for his dad, and what horrible pressure he's under, and how I intentionally turned him on with the scarf-dance thing then . . . poor guy—that wasn't fair of me at all! He shouldn't have . . . but then, I shouldn't have either.

I can't believe we talked for over two hours. Actually, it would have been more, but I told him *he* had to get some sleep.

We're going to eat lunch together on Monday and I KNOW he really does *love me*. He says he has since the first time he saw me "bouncing off the soccer field like a sunbeam." Isn't that beautiful? It's a phrase I will always keep tucked away in the most intimate part of my heart.

I'm so glad I listened to the brilliant little voice inside me that told me he was *perfect* for me . . . even when he *wasn't* so perfect. But I'm going to forget *that* part of our lives, erase it, wipe it out as though it never happened. We'll just skip over to the "and they lived happily ever after" part.

9:30 p.m.

I know I haven't written in you for two weeks, but I honestly haven't had time. Danny and I have been sooooo busy. We're together constantly when we aren't in classes or working with our teams or something, well, other than the times when Danny is working at the restaurant, which seems like it's always.

You'll like to hear this—he is really good to me, and he tells me how to act and what to wear and stuff, so he can "show me off." It makes me feel precious and adored, two of the best feelings in the world, I guess. Next week I'm going to have my hair cut in a tight little shag because that's what he thinks will look "supergreat" on me. I am happy! Happy! Happy! Happier than I've ever been in my life. Please be happy for me too!

I know *you* know that we're . . . well *it's* really part of love. Danny says before we were just "in like." I guess that's why I haven't written in you, but . . . *you're ME.* You should know everything— the good, the bad, and the ugly.

Please don't hate me for it, Daisy, or be ashamed of me or think we're wrong. I don't see how it can be wrong when it feels so right. Actually, at first it wasn't so great; in fact, it was kind of uggg, but then I found the more that I tried to please him the more I . . . but I don't want to write about that.

The worst part about Danny and I being together is the fact that I'm having to tell so many lies, lies to get to do things, then lies to cover those lies and lies to justify the lies I've covered. It's one big, horrible, getting-bigger-and-bigger circle. I'm scared to death that one day the whole thing is going to come tumbling in on me. I fear what Mom will say and do when it does. So it won't! I won't let it!

We're like Romeo and Juliet, two star-crossed lovers who are *forced* to lie because the cruel, cruel outside world can't understand the importance of our wondrous eternal love.

November 18, Saturday

1:15 a.m.

I snuck out and met Danny on the corner, and we went to a party out by the lake. It was fantastic. Everyone got smashed, and we laughed and danced and screamed and yelled and chased each other like a bunch of completely out-of-control freaks, which maybe we were, but it sure was fun. After a while we just snuggled up in pairs on blankets and became one with the universe—at least Danny and I did.

November 19, Sunday

6:15 p.m.

I'm really bored. Danny has to work both the lunch and dinner shifts because one guy quit and another hurt his foot. Jenny and Deanna and Molly have all gone to Molly's Aunt Emma's. She has a flat in the city, but Danny didn't want me to go because he hoped maybe somehow he'd get some time off in between shifts.

November 23, Thursday
Thanksgiving Day

9:03 p.m.

I knew Danny had to work all day, but I thought at least he'd phone me.

We had dinner with some of Mom's teacher friends, sort of potluck with everybody bringing something. We brought Fudge Fuffel, our favorite dessert, which was superdelicious, but I wanted Danny . . . to nibble on. He is so wonderful and beautiful and charming and witty and humorous and mannerly and personal and popular and . . . there isn't enough paper at school to write down all his amazing attributes. I am soooooooooo lucky, lucky, lucky to *have him* for my very own. I still can't imagine what WONDERFUL *HE* can see in ordinary me. BUT . . . I wish he had more control over some things; he's completely and heartbrokenly sorry afterwards, and I *do* know he's trying. I guess I'm just a ninny to expect complete perfection.

November 26, Sunday

10:20 p.m.

Danny stays tied up all the time. That means I'm really getting ahead with my school assignments.

November 30, Thursday

11:14 p.m.

At last we were alone together! It was wonderful! After school we walked for miles up Little Bear

Canyon, then sat in a flowered meadow and threw rocks in a stream. After a while Danny got excited, and we accidentally . . . uh . . . did it without a condom. I'm really worried, but I don't dare say anything. I guess I better talk to Jill, or one of the other girls we party with, about birth control pills. So far Danny isn't very careful.

December 2, Saturday

9:40 p.m.

Danny had to work again but didn't call to tell me, so I expected us to do something and stayed home all day and waited.

December 8, Friday

4:44 p.m.

Today we had our first fight. We ate lunch together in the cafeteria, and he knew I was miffed, so we walked out by the library. I said I thought he could at least call me if he'd *said he was coming over and couldn't*. He didn't answer, so I said I could go out with my friends if he couldn't make it. He called them a bunch of "sissy dweebs" and told me he didn't want me hangin' with them anymore. I jumped up and ran back into school, but even as I ran, I knew I'd do what *he* wanted. That's sad though . . . but I don't want to talk about it. I'VE MADE MY CHOICE, AND I LIKE IT!

December 15, Friday

4:41 p.m.

I left my pen on my desk at first class, and Jake Goldman came running up afterwards and gave it to me. I thanked him a lot because it was a pen my grandma had given me on my birthday. He walked me down the hall, and we talked about our grandmas for a couple of minutes. It was just a nice, polite thing to do.

At lunch Danny was furious. He accused me of "messing around" with Jake in a very loud voice. It was so embarrassing. I started crying. Immediately he put his arm around me and apologized profusely. Other people were looking at us, and I felt proud. *Humiliated* but proud, too, in some crazy-mixed-up way. Danny is each day treating me more like property he owns. I hate the way it makes me feel, but I also feel like he's sharing his power with me, his status, his car, and even his family's mansion.

Wow! I'm embarrassed. I just reread that last paragraph and it sounds like I'm the biggest phony baloney in the world and a gold digger with no ethics on top of that. I don't know how I could have written those things; *none* of them are *true*! I love Danny strictly because he is the most wonderful, gentle, loving, gorgeous hunk ever created, and I'd love him just as much if he was poor and skinny and unpopular. But . . . he's not.

10:31 p.m.

Dear Diary:
  Sometimes I'm soooooo confused and hurt and angry with Danny—no, it's *me*—I'm angry mostly with myself. I wish I could talk to you, or Mom, or someone but . . . forget it, I'll . . . I don't know what I'll do.
  How can life be both so good and so crappy at the same time? Danny being jealous about me just means he *likes* me!

December 18, Monday

1:45 a.m.

I can't believe it's just two weeks before Christmas and I KNOW I haven't really confided anything to you for a long time, but Mom and *you* don't want to hear about what's really going on in my life . . . like . . . well . . . sex. *That's* what I *need* to talk about mainly. The girls in Danny's crowd talk about IT all the time and actually . . . I'm getting as bad as they are . . . it's scary . . . like there's nothing else of importance in life, nothing else to do or think about.

Oh Daisy, in some dreary, crazy way, *I'm so unhappy*. But how can I be unhappy when I'm sooooo happy? Probably it's because Danny's friends are having such a bad influence on us. Everybody is so rude and crude, it's disgusting, and to be very truthful I don't feel good about *them* or *it* anymore. Both the girls and the guys are a horrible influence on Danny, and I wish like anything I could get him away from them, but there doesn't seem to be any way! He's so caught up with them—it's like we're one big pack of privileged gutter rats hooked on things that we know in our hearts aren't good and right—*at least I know that*! Danny's so brainwashed that he just gets completely out of control every time I even try to mention changing our lives. I know I've got to be patient to get him away from their influence. Maybe I'll even have to put up with their shit—I'm sorry, but even our language is gutter gook—anyway, maybe I'll have to stand by him till the end of next semester. Then he'll be going to high school, and surely the kids there will be more mature and stable and common sensed, don't you think?

Dearest, dear, dear Daisy, I'm so thankful and grateful that you aren't all put out of shape about what I've been telling you, and I'm proud of you that you aren't giving me hell and everything. It's such a relief to have someone to talk to who is more rational about my life than I am right now, and *maybe* I *need* someone to give me hell!

It's hard, Daisy; it's really, really hard, trying to keep up with my schoolwork to make Mom happy and trying to do all the partying and stuff with Danny to keep him happy. And . . . I don't know if I should tell you this stuff, but . . . I HAVE GOT TO TELL SOMEONE! Please, please Daisy listen, and be understanding of me . . . at least be compassionate.

I'm still such a little-kid baby in so many ways, like, for instance, here I am supposedly on "the pill" that Danny's friend gets for me, and he keeps bugging me about taking them every day when I should, but how can I remember to take the friggin' pill when I couldn't even remember to feed my cat regularly before she got run over? And I know that Danny would probably beat the shit out of me if he knew I missed sometimes, and oh, Daisy, I hate to tell you this, but he hits me a lot. When I try to talk to him about it, he always says the man is the dominant one in a relationship, so I can take it or leave it, and I *can't* leave him, Daisy, honest truly I can't! I know his creep friends would *surely ruin* his life for good without my influence. And besides he's so *truly, truly* sorry after he's lost control.

I better let us both get some sleep.

HEY, THANKS FOR LISTENING AND NOT CONDEMNING. I AM GOING TO GET THINGS STRAIGHTENED OUT, AND *YOUR HELP* IS GOING TO *HELP ME*!!!!!!

11:21 p.m.

Tonight Mom and I saw a Christmas pageant on TV, and I'm feeling so stressed out and tense and mixed-up. I'm about to climb the walls. I know a lot of things I'm doing aren't right, but I honestly don't know how I can make a change in my life until Danny is ready to, too.

Now Daisy, I'm going to talk to you about something that may shock you, but I need your common sense. Are you ready?

"Yes."

Lately Danny is sometimes hurting me A LOT during sex. He says it gives him pleasure to rough it up, and if I'm really his woman, I'll *want* to do anything that "pleasures him." I talked to Liz (one of our crowd), and she says it's a guy thing that all of the studs are into, but I still think it's sick, and I can't see how it has a single thing to do with LOVE. Oh, Daisy, tell me what to do?

"Flush him."

I can't do that Daisy. You know I can't.

"I KNOW YOU CAN."

Then you're so stupid, I don't know why I even talked to you about something so serious. You don't have a sissy clue!

3:30 p.m.

Mom's gone to church. She asked me to go with her, but I feel so dirty and unworthy, there's no way I could. I said I don't feel good. I guess that's accurate enough in the sense that I don't feel *good enough*!

I'm sorry I talked to you the way I did last night. I guess I was just trying to cover my own guilt and dirtiness by cutting you down. Forgive me?

"Sure."

I guess you're the only true friend I've got left. I'm not really comfortable with Liz and Demi, and Danny's other friends. I go with them sometimes because he doesn't want me to go with Jenny and Molly and Deanna. He calls them "Baby Chickenshits." It makes me so mad, I want to hit him, but *I know* what would happen if I did!

Anyway, now at Christmastime I'm feeling so bad and sad, when always before the season has made me feel glad and excited. Is it just because I've grown out of the little kid, Santa Claus stage, or is it because . . . am I committing adultery? Since I'm not an adult and married, *can* I commit adultery? Can't you help me? I know you can't because

. . . I don't know why because. But I do know, committing adultery is one of the "do nots" in the ten commandments. I looked that up in the encyclopedia when I first saw the movie.

How can it be that this is almost Christmas and I should be feeling "Joy to the World," when actually I'm feeling that life isn't worth living?

7:30 p.m.

NOW Christmas is really Christmas! Mom answered the door and it was guess who? Danny! She asked him in, and he was so polite and dressed up, he looked like the Prom King or something. Anyway, she invited him in, and he introduced himself and talked politely to her for a while then gave me a big gold-wrapped package. I started to unwrap it, and he slapped my hand gently and playful. "Mrs. Murphy, make her put it under the tree till tomorrow morning."

We all laughed, and Danny acted shy as he left.

"I think some nice young boy's got a crush on you," Mom said teasingly as she hugged me.

I hugged her back, not ever wanting to let go. I've been treating her so rudely for the last few months that I don't know how she can stand me. Why she doesn't send me to the "people pound"? If she only knew what that "nice young boy" was really like and how he had changed *my* life!

11:07 p.m.

Mom and I made chocolate chip cookies and ate them practically as fast as we pulled them out of the oven; then we curled up in front of the fireplace on the floor and watched the lights twinkle on the Christmas tree and saw a Christmas movie on the VCR. It was like the olden days when I was a little kid, and I wanted it to stay that way forever.

December 25, Monday
Christmas Day

2:13 a.m.

Time has stopped dead in its tracks. Hurry, hurry, hurry. I want it to be morning so I can open Danny's present and of course Mom's, but most of all, DANNY'S! What in the world could it ever be? Mom let me smell it and shake it and pinch it a smidge, but she wouldn't let me tear the paper the littlest bit.

10:21 a.m.

At 5:?? a.m. I simply couldn't stand it another second, so I tiptoed down the hall and crawled into bed with Mom, like I used to do with Mom and

Dad when I was tiny. She snuggled up close, snorted, and pretended to snore, until we got the giggles; then we jumped out of bed and raced in by the tree just like in the long-ago fairy-tale days of our life.

Guess what was in the *big* box? A smaller box, then a smaller box, and a smaller box after that, until it was getting so small, I had one moment of wondering if it was going to be just a sick, hurtful joke.

"Open it, open it." Mom laughed. She could do that because she just knew the *outside* Danny.

With trembling fingers I ripped away the last bits of heavily taped paper and there . . . I'm crying all over you . . . was the sweetest little plain bracelet I had ever seen. On it was inscribed, beside one little flower, which looked something like a cross between a dandelion and a rose (but maybe that was just in my eyes), anyway, it said, "HI, FRIEND." Enough, huh? More than enough!

It's a good thing I didn't know where Danny's grandma lives (he and his Dad had gone there to spend a couple of days); if I had, I'd have been on the phone in a minute.

7:45 p.m.

Christmas was gentle and sweet. I went to service with Mom and truly, truly, deeply, deeply repented while I was there, but . . . I don't know how long that's going to last; maybe if I'm very, very lucky, I can make Danny see all the wonders of . . . I dunno . . . those things are pretty hard to put into words.

December 31, Sunday
New Year's Eve

9:15 p.m.

Mom's going to a big New Year's Eve party with some of the school people she works with because she thinks I'm going to spend the night with Jenny. I hope nothing horrible happens that makes her have to call Jenny's because Danny and I are going to spend our first New Year's together. I know Jenny will lie for us if she has to.

January 1, Monday
New Year's Day

10:59 a.m.

I'm so weak, I can't believe it! I tried for about *one minute* to be straight and virtuous, then the music and the energy and the beer and . . . other stuff, took over. . . .

"Who let them take over?"

Oh, *SHUT UP* your pages. How could you know how enticing those things are?

"I know."

No, you don't! You couldn't possibly have the least inkling!!!!!! I'd been away from Danny for so long, even I couldn't believe the animalistic powers and urges I had.

"What about the 'Vow of Chastity Until Marriage' you made with the Bible Group when you were on the outing? And what about all those promises you made when you went to Christmas service?"

Excuse my tears, but they mean I'm a weak-kneed, lying, lily-livered, flopping fool with no control . . . no morals . . . no ethics . . . and that . . . that . . .

"That what?"

I've gone so far I'll . . . never . . . be able to come back.

"Don't close the page, Annie! . . ."

I have to.

January 4, Thursday

9:49 p.m.

Danny sees me only when *HE* wants to see me. We do only what *he* wants to do when *he* wants to do it. I wanted him to come to my soccer game in Santa Marina, but NO he has things to do with the guys. I'm getting pretty damn sick and tired of the way he treats me. It's the shits. And he *lies* to me—I wonder if he just lies to me about some things—or about *everything*! Can he possibly know or care how insecure and unimportant he often makes me feel?

January 6, Saturday

12 noon exactly

I sneaked out last night and we partied till I sneaked in about 2 a.m. Danny was so good to me that he wiped out all the bad feelings I've been having. I guess I'm really selfish expecting him to be perfect. Someday when we're out of high school and in college, he'll be mature enough to put *my* things a little higher on *his* category list. I've got to be patient and accept and appreciate the wonders of *him*, and I don't most of the time. I just hope someday he'll do the same for me.

I worry a little because Danny doesn't have, or doesn't want to wear condoms and . . . you know how I sometimes can't remember if I've taken my pill or not. I think I do, and I usually do, at least most of the time I do, but it's such a dumb, everyday drag.

Think I'll go back to sleep. I feel like shit.

January 8, Monday

9:45 p.m.

Danny and I cut school for the whole day and went bird-watching. It was awesome with us hiking and pretending we were shipwrecked on a deserted land, and the only two known people alive. Actually, after we'd eaten the lunch I'd brought, we broke boughs off a big old, dead oak tree and made ourselves a little hut. It was a fun and an exciting Robinson Crusoe-type adventure. I loved it! Loved it! Loved it! I wish we didn't ever have to go to school ever again, that we could just do things like that every day.

January 13, Saturday

9:20 a.m.

I'm sooooo happy, I think I'm going to die. Last night Danny and I saw an old, old movie at his house. It was the dearest, cleanest, most loving and gentle film I'd ever seen, about ethics and caring for each other even when things were down, and of course, it had a happy ending. We both agreed after it was over that we wanted our lives to be just like that, and they will be. I can feel it in my bones, whatever that means.

January 14, Sunday

9:47 p.m.

I know I haven't been keeping you up on school stuff. So—both Danny and I have been in state run-offs: he in football, me in soccer. We're like "ships crossing in the halls" or whatever that silly saying is. Anyway, Daisy, I need to talk to you. I know it's dumb and all like that . . . and I don't even want to think about it . . . but . . . well, I've missed my period. Now don't go jumping to crazy conclusions; you know as well as I do that I'm sometimes irregular, and besides I take the pill . . . well, usually . . . and Danny . . . sometimes . . . oh, I'm just being dumb, dumb, DUMB; *that* couldn't happen to me. Truthfully, though . . . last month . . . I just kind of spotted . . . but not to worry. WE WON'T WORRY! It's going to be all right. Right? I'm sure it's just because I've been so busy and under such sports pressure and stuff. In health class the teacher once said that stress could cause irregularity. WE WILL NOT THINK ABOUT IT AGAIN. AND FROM NOW ON, I'M GOING TO BE VERY, VERY, CAREFUL!!!!!!!

January 16, Tuesday

6:02 a.m.

Last night we were over at Tina's. Mom thought I was studying late at the library. Tina's mom works nights at Rhodies, so we had the house to ourselves. Danny and Kip were playing pool, and Tina and I were fixing some munchies in the kitchen, when suddenly she sat down and held her hands to her head tight. I hurried to help her and asked what was the matter. I certainly didn't expect her to blurt out that she'd just had an abortion two days before, and she still wasn't feeling too cool.

The words struck me like lightning, and all the pictures I'd ever seen in health classes flipped through my mind. Tiny little fetus babies smaller than your little finger, wiggling around and then . . . being killed . . . sucked out of you like they were . . . I couldn't stand to think about it, and I started crying. Tina tried to comfort me but she didn't understand that I wasn't crying for her as much as I was crying for that sad little boy or girl baby that had just been thrown away like it was junk.

I couldn't think about anything else all night long. Tina's just a year older than I am, so she couldn't have had a baby—at least she shouldn't have, but—I don't know . . . I'm feeling so lost and scared and lonely empty.

January 23, Tuesday

4:47 p.m.

It's been a week or so since I told you . . . you know . . . but it's maybe okay now because yesterday I started spotting a little. I'm *so* glad and relieved and SAVED! It was really scary—Tina telling me about her abortion right after I'd begun to wonder about . . . well, at least *that's over*! I hope, I hope, I hope! I hate this being so irregular.

I'm going to do some serious mature rethinking about my life. I don't like the filthy, trashy talking we do when we're partying and some of the things that go on, like a few weeks ago when the guys were goading Tina and Kaytie to wrestle in their underwear, then trying to get them to wrestle nude.

We're not setting ourselves up as very good future-parent material.

I wonder how many of the girls beside Tina in our crowd have had abortions? They're the cheerleaders and such that most other girls at school think they would like to be like. (If they only knew!)

I think I'm going to talk to Danny about making some changes in *our* lives. Maybe I should even think about . . . NO, I can't do *that*; I don't want to! I won't! I'm not sure I could make it *without him*!

January 25, Thursday

8:26 p.m.

Mom's at a school board meeting. I'm bored out of my skull. Schoolwork used to be fun and a challenge. I know I sometimes nagged and moaned and groaned about having to do it, but it still gave me a good feeling when I finished an assignment. It's been a gloomy glucky day. I wish I could be with Danny, but the football team has been in a slump, and the coach practically has them living at the field when they're not in school. I RESENT THAT, and I'm getting nasty and more mean-spirited about it *all the time*! I seem to be coming *first* on everybody's shit list these days. It's not fair; in fact, it's a hell of a way to live; a shitty, hellish way.

February 10, Saturday

8:20 a.m.

Danny's working all weekend.

10:17 a.m.

It's about time for my period again, and I'm looking forward to it and counting the days like it was Christmas coming up, except not a happy Christmas, maybe the saddest and most somber Christmas of my life. Each day I've been becoming more morbid and I know that's positively idiotic because . . . because what? I won't think about it! I ABSOLUTELY, POSITIVELY WILL *NOT* THINK ABOUT IT. I WILL NOT!!!!!!!!!!!

February 14, Wednesday

3:51 p.m.

What a VALENTINE'S DAY! I brought a sack lunch for two, and Danny and I ate at the bottom of the stairs behind the heat vent. He gave me a heart-shaped necklace and I gave him a heart-shaped key chain ... AND I DIDN'T THINK ABOUT *IT* ONE BIT ... WELL, HARDLY ONE BIT. I wish I could talk to Danny about it ... but why talk about it when I'm not even sure? Actually ...

I know I'm not. I can't be! I'm only two days late, and I'm not always regular, but ... what if? Last month I only had spot bleeding. I think I'm going to put on my rollerblades and go way down to the other side of town where no one could possibly know me and buy one of those home test kits. I wonder if they have simple directions that stupid me can understand. On TV they seem simple enough for a primate to figure out.

4:15 p.m.

Danny called, but I pretended I was sick. I am sick!! I AM SICK AND SCARED AND TIRED OF ALL THE SHITTY SHITTYNESS IN MY LIFE!

5:10 p.m.

Mom has to go to the market, and as soon as I hear the front door close, I'm going to do it. Even *knowing* can't be worse than this waiting. Ohhhhhhhhhh I am soooooooooooo scared, so white-knuckled, heart-in-my-throat, head-throbbing-like-it's-going-to-explode SCARED WITLESS. Maybe it's better if I don't know. But what if? Oh, time, time, time pass. Mom get out, go, go, go.

6:01 p.m.

The complete bottom has fallen out of my world; the blackness of night and Satan and everything evil and scary in creation is pulling in on me. My tears bathe your pages in the sorrow and pain of the anguished. I CANNOT BEAR TO FACE IT! I WILL NOT! But

what else

can I do?

It *was* Pink!

I am soooooooooooooooooooooo depressed and forlorn.

I would ask God to help me, but in no way am I worthy of calling on Him for help. I didn't think I needed Him when I was out doing what I wanted to do without worrying, or even thinking about "consequences for actions." NO, *stupid me*, I thought I could have all of life's fun and games without paying any price, buying any tickets, taking any responsibility. What an asshole . . . See, I've allowed myself to become so comfortable with unacceptable language that I'm not even aware when I'm using it. What a liar and a cheat and a trashbin gutter guppie I've become.

I wish I had a . . . no, I don't. Escaping with any of that stuff would just prolong the whole shitty . . . see, I've done it again, my mouth has become as corrupt as my body and my soul, whatever the hell that means.

How am I ever going to tell Mom? I'm going to *have* to tell her sometime. Will she cry? Will she scream? Will it break her heart? Will she want me to . . . leave . . . or?

Oh, I'm so mixed up, and I'm hurting with a kind of hurt I didn't even know existed! It's a *million times* more than when I had my hand slammed in the car door and had to go to the emergency room. Then I was writhing and screaming, and now it's all that with mind, heart, *religious* pain, and guilt mixed in.

I DON'T WANT THIS RESPONSIBILITY! I'M ONLY FOURTEEN! I CAN'T HANDLE IT! It's like I'm lost in an evil forest and there are monsters and beasts that I've never heard of, trying to get me. I want to be a little kid again snuggled up safe and warm in my mama's arms, with no problems.

How am I ever going to tell Danny? I'm afraid to my bones, really, really afraid. I know *he'll* scream at me . . . maybe . . . No, he wouldn't hit me when I was . . . I can't even say the word—

I once saw what a pressure cooker does when it explodes. That's exactly how I feel, just one second from having my brains dangling from the ceiling and my lungs and guts plastered to the doors and walls.

But why am I being so damn morbid? Often those stupid tests *aren't* correct! I better buy another one and try it again. Chances are I didn't even do it right the first time.

6:12 p.m.

Mom thinks I'm going rollerblading. She warned me that it's going to be dark soon, and I should be extra, extra careful so that something bad doesn't happen to me. Something *BAD*? How much worse could it get?

6:43 p.m.

I'm back and I can't believe how much this junk costs—$15 a kit, 2 for $30. 'Bye-bye allowance! Won't Mom *ever* go to bed? I don't dare go in the bathroom to use these crazy things till I know she's asleep, then I have to sneak down to the trash can behind the carports to dispose of the evidence.

February 15, Thursday

3:33 a.m.

Of course, *you* know the test was pink again! But please, please, please don't dump on me! I'm about as fragmented as I can be without collapsing into a pile of dust. I wish I could do that! I truly do wish I could!

4:12 a.m.

I've cried until there are literally no more tears left in me, not one single one. I sob and sniff, and it's like dry, hot, hard rocks tear out of my eye socket; not soft, wet, cool ones. And they're like acid burning, stinging, flesh-eating acid.

7:01 a.m.

I guess I finally dry-cried myself to sleep because Mom has been pounding at my door for what seems like hours. It seemed like the noise was coming from a far-away other planet.

8:15 a.m.

Mom is really worried about me. She said I look like a ghost, and she wants to take me to the doctor. I don't know how I can get around that, but I guess the old "flu" thing may work. She's gone to get me a fresh pillow because mine was soaked. She thinks I had a fever, but that it's broken. She's made me promise I'll call her at school if the slightest little change takes place in my condition.

I WISH!!!!!!!!!!!!!!!!!!!!!!!!!!!!!!!!!!!!!
!!!!!!!!!!!!!!!!!!!!!!
!!!!!!!!!!

4:31 p.m.

Mom called school and had me paged during lunchtime. She's treating me like a five-year-old. Once I almost blurted out to her what was wrong with me when she was giving me the old goo-goo, goo-goo stuff. Of course, I didn't though. I know she senses something is *really really* wrong, and I have no clue as to how I'm going to face telling her. Maybe I should talk to Tina first. Oh, I will, I will! I'm glad I thought of that. She's been through the whole thing. I feel better already. Not *good* by a long shot, but at least able to get up and be mobile. I'll call Tina as soon as I'm sure she's home from school. She's got to come *straight* home today! She's got to!

5:55 p.m.

Tina met me at Ritter's Park, and we talked for almost an hour, but it hasn't made me feel any better. She's so, so, so different than I am! She didn't even tell Kip she was . . . you know, and she didn't tell her mom either. Marcie arranged for her to have the abor—I still get sick to my stomach and my all-over when I think about that. She tried to convince me that before the third month *the fetus isn't an anything.* I hope she's right, but it doesn't seem to me that's what the nurse at school showed us and told us. Maybe I'm wrong. Wouldn't it be wonderful if I am wrong and Tina is right?

Actually I think Tina messed me up more than ever. I wish I'd never talked to her, but then I *wish* a lot of things right now!

6:30 p.m.

Mom said she tried to call me after school, before she stopped at the market for some special things I like. When I didn't answer, she presumed I was either asleep or in the bathroom, thank goodness for that!

Danny phoned. I'm so disconbooberated that I told him I was SERIOUSLY GROUNDED, for I didn't know how long, and I'm not allowed to even use the phone. He seemed more sad than pissed like I thought he'd be. He can be sooooo sweet!

February 17, Saturday

I'm going crazy. REALLY TRULY GOING CRAZY! I think Danny suspects what's happening because I've been doing everything in the book to avoid him. And Mom? I just stay in my room and say I'm trying to catch up on my studies and that I'm having PMS. PMS? Huh! I wish! Thank goodness they're doing some remodeling at Mom's school, and she's having to teach late extra classes, so she comes home late and wrung out.

Me: in the past, I've been lying and doing everything else that's bad, and I've been getting away with it, but ... now ... being ... you know ... there's no way I can hide *that*. Actually I may be two months pregnant. *THERE*, I SAID THE WORD *PREGNANT*, SO IT'S REAL!

I've been denying it for so long that it's almost a relief in some masochistic way to have it out. I've pretended my breasts *weren't* a little tender, and that I just had an upset stomach ... I'm such a phony! But *now it's "Pay-up time!"* Shall I do what Tina did? I'm not sure I can. I mean I'm not sure I can get those pictures of the squirming little semi-human things floating around out of my mind. But having a baby myself—I don't think so! I remember watching Francie, who finally had to quit school because the kids were giving her such a hard time. Ugg, this really is a choice between a rock and a hard place.

February 20, Tuesday

1:22 a.m.

Three days have passed since I found out the news. I still haven't been able to face it enough to go back to school, but I guess tomorrow I'll have to choose between school and the doctor, some choice. MOM CAN BE SUCH AN ASS SOMETIMES.

1:23 a.m.

The telephone number of the anti-abortion office just flashed up on my mind like a huge red neon sign. It was weird, almost like a spooky omen or something. Then I remembered that the anti-abortion lady who had talked on TV one time had had a big banner with huge red numbers printed across it, hanging behind her on the stage, so the night vision of whatever it was probably didn't mean beans, but *anyway*, just to be sure, I immediately got up and wrote it down.

2:01 a.m.

I've got to, I'VE SIMPLY GOT TO maturely and rationally work this problem out! It's not like leaving one of my rollerblades in the park or forgetting to give one of my teachers a note or something. Ummmm. Should I go to Planned Parenthood first to learn all about the truths of abortion, or to the anti-abortion people or . . . maybe some church person, not someone Mom knows for sure, but . . . I feel like Alice in Wonderland: everything is getting curiouser and curiouser by the second, and I'm getting more lost and more lost in the rabbit holes; and the stupid Cheshire Cat won't tell me anything about the keys to the big door and the little door and . . .

How could I ever take care of a baby—I couldn't even remember to change my cat's litter box and feed and water her half of the time—remember?

I just woke myself up shivering and whimpering. It was the most realistic and horrifying experience I have ever had in my life! So real I can still feel the . . . but let me tell you from the beginning because it wasn't like a dream at all! In some demented way I think it *actually happened*! I remember *every* detail, the blood on the doctor's coat . . . Whoa, back up.

First I called the doctor Tina told me about. His nurse said to come in at 1:30.

With fear and trembling I dressed, went to the bank, and drew out money from my savings, then took the A bus to River Road, a kind of run-down part of town. A storm was just beginning to blow in, and trash and dirt gusted around my legs. In the waiting room there were four other girls, all about my age. Only one had her mother with her, a heavily made-up, tense-looking, sullen woman. Two of the girls were escorted through the small door into nowhere by a burly looking Amazon-type woman in white. Before *Days Of Our Lives* was over on the tiny television in the office, the first girl was led back. The Amazon called my name then, and my legs felt like cooked spaghetti as I got up and tried to follow her.

I was put on a cold metal table with only a sheet

of paper under me, and I will forever feel the cold, hard tongs pulling the baby out of me and throwing it into a huge wastebin with a plastic liner. They had given me a shot like Tina had said they would, but it hadn't taken, for some reason, and I don't know why they didn't use the vacuum thing.

After the procedure I took the longest, darkest, coldest bus trip home I had ever taken, and I know this sounds crazier than crazy, but I HONESTLY DO FEEL LIKE I'VE REALLY HAD THE ABORTION AND IT'S ALL OVER! Do you think that's possible? That through some kind of science fiction thing I . . . OHHHHHH, I've never done this before, but I'm going to go take one of the sleeping pills Dr. Harmon gave Mom when she sprained her ankle . . . No, I'll take two. . . . I've *got* to escape from this . . . crazed cage I've imprisoned myself into.

I wish I hadn't talked to Tina, or at least that she hadn't told me all the *gory details*. I'm not handling things like that very well these days.

February 22, Thursday

3:14 p.m.

I *really did* go talk to the clinic people. They were nice, but . . . I guess I shouldn't have talked to Tina first . . . and maybe the dream got me off balance.

Anyway, I've had little Whosit in my belly for over two months (I forgot to ask how they really count when they don't know), and I remember how lonely I felt for *her* coming home on the bus after my dream abortion. Oh, I am soooooooooo sick . . . sick . . . sick . . . probably *terminally mentally ill*! I just had a horrible thought. What if I'm programming my baby with my sick, morbid thoughts? Wouldn't that be a terrible unforgivable thing? But if she's just clumps of cells now . . . but I don't think she is! Actually, the books say she looks like a teeny one- or two-inch real baby, and she's swimming around in there in that a—am—whatever fluid, like a baby . . . then she must be a . . . FISH. Now I *know* I'm totally, totally insane! I wonder if being pregnant and having your body chemicals change around, like they told us in health class, could possibly make someone's brain stop working all together.

I wish . . . *I wish* . . . I *wish* I had someone to talk to before my mind splatters all over the room. I'm hurting so bad, I don't know how much more I can take. The hairs on my head ache. My toenails hurt. I'm desperate. I wish there was some way I could just quit living.

Die?

I've always been afraid of dying before, but . . . maybe it's soft and warm and floating and dark and no-thinking forever . . .

I don't think I'd like that!

What about Heaven?

Heaven sounds good, but I'm not sure people who commit suicide can go to Heaven, *especially if* they KILL their absolutely, totally innocent little growing baby along with them.

Then there's Hell? I don't know much about Hell, but it sounds like *hell*. That attempt at humor was pathetic. I'm pathetic! And I am sooooooooooo tired, it's an effort to breathe. What shall I do? What shall I ever do?

"You can talk to Mom?"

Now *you're* even crazier than I am. Why would I want to hurt her like I'm hurting? She's not responsible for any of my stupidity and suffering. She doesn't need to be involved in my . . .

"Yes, she does."

No, she doesn't!

"Yes, she does! Hasn't she helped you out of every other hole you've gotten yourself into in the past?"

But nothing, NOTHING I've ever done in the past compares with this! Have you ever considered the *lifetime, forever* complications a baby involves? The problems . . .

"You know very well that problems *DO NOT go away* by *ignoring them*! Get real! *You can't* handle this big one without Mom's help. No way can you handle it."

But what will she think of me? She'll hate me. She'll be sorry she ever had me.

"What other choice do you have at this point?"

I guess you're right. Maybe tomorrow—next month—next never-day.

"WHAT ABOUT RIGHT NOW?"

I can't! I can't! I CAN'T! . . . but maybe I can . . . no, I can't! I won't! So there!!!!!!!!

6:15 p.m.

Danny called. I pretended I had laryngitis. I don't know why I *can't* talk to him when I want to and *need* to talk to him more than anything in the world! His team is playing Torrance and Bayfield, so they'll be gone tomorrow and Saturday. He hangs up when Mom answers.

February 23, Friday

Today I finally forced myself to go back to school, but I'm held together by a thread. I keep thinking if one person said anything out of the ordinary, I would either scream or cry.

I must be sending out weird vibrations or something because no one tried to bug me like I thought they would. I thought honestly that everyone would see my problem like the scarlet letter on Hester's dress. And they'd all be giggling and talking behind my back wondering what I was going to do.

Danny and some of the guys passed me in the hall between science and English, and for a moment my heart almost burst with joy as *he* gave me a quick hug and whispered in my ear that he hoped I was being a really, really good girl, so I'd soon be "ungrounded." Then he winked and said, "I *need* you," as he dashed off. I could feel myself blushing because I knew the guys knew, as well as I did what he meant.

Jake pushed Danny as he yelled over his shoulder, "Don't get *too* eager because he's ours for the next week or so. We've got practice and traveling games up to our kazoos."

I just waved self-consciously.

February 29, Thursday

4:46 p.m.

I haven't talked to you for about a week, but I couldn't! I don't have anything to say, and yet in some crazy way, I've got miles and miles and hours and hours of talking I want to do. I want to talk to Mom with all my soul. I want to have her hug me and tell me everything is going to be all right and that I'm not absolutely the worst, most evil person in the world. But I feel so *scared*! What if she *won't love me anymore*? What if she kicks me out to fend for myself like I read about a mother doing to her daughter one time?

That's stupid! I know Mom loves me. No other kid has ever been more loved than I have been. I remember when she was voted FAVORITE TEACHER in the whole high school and then the state. I wanted to get up and yell that she was also the BEST MOTHER. And my grandmas love me, and my dad. I don't see them much, BUT I STILL KNOW THEY LOVE ME.

Okay, so I'm loved! NOW:

What about the . . . I've got to face it some time or another . . . I've got to say it! But I can't; I truly can't!!!!! Please say it for me, Daisy! Please!

"What about the little tadpole real-live baby that's growing inside you?"

It probably is a real tadpolelike little girl or boy baby growing right here in my belly, isn't it? But I still can't believe it. I know this happens to other females—girls, women, married, unmarried, black, white, brown, yellow, and every other color, if there are other colors—BUT, IT CAN'T BE HAPPENING TO ME! I'm only fourteen years old! I'm in junior high school, in the eighth grade! Please, please don't let it be happening to me!

But it is happening to me, and I've got to face it! I've missed two periods, which means I'M TWO MONTHS PREGNANT! MAYBE . . . even . . .

My skin is crawling. It's like I'm possessed. I've got a living thing growing inside me, about to take over my life. I don't want it there! I want to be just me again! Please, please, just me, just me.

Oh, Father, forgive me. I have sinned. Forgive me and make it not be so. But it is so! What to do? What to do?

12:47 a.m.

I can't sleep. I can't relax. I can't breathe. I can't think. But I've *got* to *do something*. I've got to tell Danny! It's going to be hard, but sooner or later he's got to face it too; I didn't get pregnant all by myself. I guess I'll leave an urgent message in his locker tomorrow first thing.

I'm totally scared to death just thinking about it but I've got to do it; I have no other choice. I won't be like Tina. I won't! I can't!

3:46 a.m.

I tried to pray like I used to do when I was little, but I couldn't. It used to be so easy and I felt so close to Heavenly Father, but now . . . I can't connect. It's like I've lost the combination to open the door. How sad and lonely and shut out I feel.

Hey, wait a minute, maybe I've just been looking for gloom and doom. WHAT IF? . . . just *what if* I talked to Danny and he . . . wanted us to get married? What if he *wants* an adorable little dress-up doll baby, a little skin-soft-as-velvet baby to coo at him and make him feel like he is the greatest creator in all of creation! What if his dad wants us to live in his beautiful big, big, big house, maybe take the east wing as our own private for-real playhouse. And Lucille, their maid, could tend little Whosit while we both went to school.

We'd get married in the garden under the big old oak tree by the river. Everybody we know would be there and . . . we'd live happily ever after just like in fairy tales.

4:49 p.m.

I think I am terminally wounded. I know I am. No one can survive this much pain, or can they? I hope so. What caused the pain? you ask. Oh, Daisy, it was so horrible, so unbelievable, sadistically horrible that I'm sure words can never describe it to you, but I'll try. Last night I wrote a note telling Danny I desperately had to see him for lunch, and I poked it through the vent in his locker this morning.

It was a nightmare from the first because when he met me in the parking lot he thought I just wanted to go to his house and "do it," like we'd sometimes done in the past, and I was too much in shock to tell him anything else.

He blabbed all the way there and didn't even notice me or my feelings, just what he was doing, and had done, and was yet going to do. At one point I wanted to reach over and scratch his eyes out for about one second, then I shrunk even deeper into myself.

Once inside his house, he made a grab for me that made me feel like I was being attacked by some alien monster. I screamed and pushed him away. In fact, I pushed him so hard he almost lost his balance. "You shouldn't have done that, Bitch," he said between clinched teeth.

I stood up to him for the first time and said coldly, "I'm not a bitch. I'm . . . I'm the mother of your unborn child."

"No way," he hissed.

The rest of it is like a movie playing and replaying in my mind.

"We've got to talk this out calmly and sanely," I said, ignoring his insults.

"There's nothing to talk about."

"There is too. I'm . . ."

"I know what you are. You're a dirty, careless 'ho.' " He slapped me so hard across the face, I could hear the bones in my neck crack, but I held my ground.

"I've been your girlfriend, and I'm pregnant! You've got to help me *decide* what to do about it."

He hit me again, this time in the stomach and yelled, "Your little bastard could be any guy in town's good-time slime."

I felt so used and degraded, I wanted with everything in me to turn and crawl away, but something stronger than myself kept me there crying and begging him and pleading for him to take some responsibility.

Finally he asked, "What in hell do you expect of me?"

That kind of threw me, and I blubbered, "Maybe . . . maybe we could get married?"

He flew into an even deeper rage. "I'm sixteen years old, duh-head. You think I'm going to stifle my life for you and your slimy little bastard?" He gagged and shuddered. "Give up football? High school? College? Parties? Freedom? Fun? No way! You probably got pregnant just trying to trap me."

I sniffled, "But . . ."

"Forget it, slut. I'm not buying into your shit. To me you're just another piece of poor-white-trash flesh trying to flush the rich kid down the toilet with you."

He pulled his arm back, and I turned so he wouldn't hit me again in the stomach. "It's your problem, bitch; *you* take care of it."

Scared out of my wits and mentally muddled and bleeding, I fell at his knees. "I'll . . . have an abortion if that's what you want."

He picked me up by one arm and dragged me to the porch. "Try your sad-ass act on some of the other guys you've done it with."

As he drove off in a grinding of gears, all I could think about was how grateful I was that at least this time I had enough money to take a bus home.

Now my problem is . . . will Mom discard me too? Maybe? Yes? No? And I've got to face another thing—Danny's a damn liar all the way—so . . . could he have given me AIDS or . . . or . . . something? Oh, how I wish I'd listened in health class so I'd know more . . . about . . . everything!! Poor me! What to do? What to do?

It's almost time for Mom to come home after her last late class, and for the first time I've felt pangs of pain for the poor little innocent, unwanted baby that is growing within me. Nobody wants it. It might as well be lying out in the middle of a busy, dark freeway in a blinding storm. It had no choice in the matter. Danny did! I did! Not it! Poor little unloved, dejected part of my body. I wish I could love it. I wonder if I can learn to? Someone needs to! It's in such a helpless, hopeless, loveless situation. Maybe I can learn to love it. I hope I can! Someone has got to! NO living thing in the world should have to live without love and *respect*, maybe *respect* even more than love!

Oh, Mom, please hurry home. I need you to help guide me through this darkest period in my life. I KNOW I've been rude and mean and disrespectful to you the last few months, when I thought Danny was the epitome of all things good and you were—I can't even write what I felt you sometimes were—*AND YOU WEREN'T*! I was the stupid asshole . . . but I'm not going to use that gutter-type language any more. It's going out with the gutter-type lifestyle I've been living. I want to be what you want me to be. I always have! I've known you only wanted the best for me, both mentally and physically, and I'm proud of you and what you've done with your life. You're an ideal example for me and for every other young person who comes across your path. Why couldn't I have tried harder to follow in your footsteps?

I hear Mom coming in the front door, and I'm literally frozen in my tracks. Will she understand? Can she? Will she still respect and love me after I tell her?

WELL,

HERE

GOES NOTHING!

March 2, Saturday

2:30 a.m.

I can't believe my Mom! As soon as she put down the groceries and stuff she'd brought home from school, I took her by the hand and led her into the living room and just blurted out the whole truth. She didn't scold or nag or scream or show me to the door or any of the other cruel and terrible things I'd thought had been possibilities. She just kept saying over and over quietly, "It's going to be all right, baby. You and I together can handle it." Her soft, warm hands holding mine tightly made me know that we could.

After I'd told her all that I thought was necessary, not about Danny beating on me or anything like that, she held me as she had when I was a child and told me how "eternally precious" I was to her. Then suddenly she stood up, wiped away both her tears and mine and looked me straight in the eye and said, "Now it's time for us to *get on* with our lives. Let's go fix dinner, then go for a long walk to prove to ourselves that *we* are both in charge! As we walk and after we get home, we'll talk until we've made some comfortable solutions for at least the next couple of days." She squeezed me so tightly, I winced. "After that, we'll take it one easy step at a time, right?"

"Right," I whispered back.

After our long, long, long, long walk and our even longer talk, she drew a warm bath for me, then sat on the side of my bed and gently rubbed my back and shoulders and neck till I fell asleep.

How could she be so *good* to me when I have been so terrible to her?

I wonder what we're going to do about my little tadpole? I can see it just like the pictures on the screen—teeny, tiny hands and arms and legs and big head wiggling in the amble—something fluid. I hope . . . I really do hope I don't have to . . . but I'll do what Mom thinks we should, or rather what we together think is best for the three of us. Oh dear, I've got to quit thinking of *it* as a her; it will make it too hard if I have to . . .

March 4, Monday

4:32 p.m.

Mom and I talked all weekend like I wish we'd done, and we should have done, months ago. Then today she suggested that I go to school as usual. She knows it won't be easy, but life goes on even if I am . . . you know. She was right and I can't believe how *normal* everything around me seems while I inside feel so . . . so . . . unnormal. At least it doesn't seem exactly normal to me, for a fourteen-year-old kid to be going around with another even littler kid developing inside her guts. It's sort of science fiction or something, but maybe not.

8:22 p.m.

Mom suggested after dinner when we were talking, and we talk a *lot* these days, that she make an appointment for me to see a doctor. I agreed, but it's going to be so embarrassing and make everything so absolutely final.

6:06 p.m.

We just got home from Doctor Stewart's. He's Mom's friend, and he worked us into his schedule as soon as she called. He says I appear to be almost *three* months pregnant, and I should make a decision *immediately* as to what I'm going to do about my pregnancy. *THERE*! I've used the P-word again and it didn't kill me, but . . . what about the fetus? No one yet calls it a baby, except me, and maybe I shouldn't, but I can't help thinking of it as one. I guess we're all different, and we have a right to think what we please. For instance, Tina, she obviously didn't think at all about her baby fetus being a baby, but me—well, I'm me.

I'm going to do what Mom wants, but . . . life is sometimes really difficult, isn't it? But at least I've got good old Mom to help me through it. I am sooooooooo lucky!

9:20 p.m.

Mom and I have talked it over carefully and have decided to make a final decision in the next couple of days. Dr. Stewart says it isn't wise to wait much after that. I do, but I don't! NO. I don't, but I do. I really . . . I don't know. . . .

> *Oh sleep, dear sleep*
> *Come to me soon*
> *And rock me gently, quietly*
> *In the cradle of the moon.*

I hope tomorrow never comes. The decision is too final!

March 6, Wednesday

4:31 p.m.

School is becoming harder every day. I don't *belong anywhere anymore.* I'm not a kid and I'm not an adult. Danny stays out of my way like I have the plague. I bet he's told everybody and their gossipy aunt about my being what I am, saying he's not any part of it.

I *don't want* to go with Danny's friends anymore, and my old friends don't seem to *want* to go with me. But why should they? I cut them out cold when Danny told me to. How foolish, foolish, foolish I've been in a million different ways.

I wonder if I'll *ever* be able to put all the pieces back together again. Now I know what the Humpty Dumpty children's poem really means!

March 7, Thursday

7:59 a.m.

Mom and I got up real early and sat on our little friendly balcony and had breakfast and watched the sun come up. I dared to tell her how I felt about the little squiggly growing inside me, and she said she felt the same way, but she hadn't wanted to force me to do something I might regret. We hugged each other and said together, quietly and happily, "We're going to have a baby! We're going to have a baby! We're going to have a baby!" Then I started singing softly, "We're going to *love our* baby." And Mom joined in, "We're going to *love our* baby. We're going to *love our* baby." It was a really moving moment.

Mom knows how superduper-super sorry I am to have gotten myself into this predicament, especially at such a young age. She's sorry, too, from the bottom of her soul, but she didn't condemn me or berate me or anything hurtful. She just stands firmly at my side now that THIS IS THE WAY IT IS.

Gotta run catch the bus,
> Bye,

See ya tonight! You're about my only friend left. Thank you for being my *true, trusted and always there friend*!

March 14, Thursday

9:42 p.m.

I know I haven't written in you for a long time, but life is very difficult for me now. I have to live out every minute with apprehension. I'm so paranoid that the kids will somehow know and judge and condemn me, and I also suspect the teachers know and are reviewing me as a bad example. In a way I wish I could drop out of school, but of course that is *not* an option. How could I ever get into high school and then college without a junior high school diploma? Besides, I want an education. I know *that* is the only way to become independent and earn a decent living.

4:34 p.m.

Danny passed in the hall just as I was coming out of the library, and his eyes got *absolutely blank*. It was as though he was looking right at me, but totally *through me* like I was invisible.

I turned around, went back into the library, and hid behind a bookshelf and cried for a couple of minutes till I got myself together.

It was so humiliating and demeaning! How could I ever have thought he was God's gift to the world? He's just a *selfish, self-centered, arrogant, brutal animal*, or did I just bring out the ugliness and degeneracy in him? I don't think so! In fact I remember Kip laughingly saying one time when Tina was crying that "If it didn't hurt, I wasn't doing it right," and all the guys laughing with him.

I wish I could talk to Mom about *that* kind of stuff, but I can't. I do wish I could, though, because something tells me that *real love* isn't about being hurtful at all.

I just looked up LOVE IN BOTH THE DICTIONARY AND THE THESAURUS AND IT MEANS SHARING, CARING, GIVING, RESPECT, GOOD THINGS AND ON AND ON. I don't think Danny and his gang even know what the word

"LOVE" means! It certainly doesn't mean beating up on girls or making them like semislaves.

March 16, Saturday

4:33 p.m.

I'm different now! I don't belong anywhere! It's sort of like I'm a mutant. No one is comfortable with me and I'm not comfortable with them or myself. Mom tries to do everything she can to make me . . . at least a *little bit* secure. Sometimes she tries too hard, and it puts me even more out of the circle of humanity. That miffs me so much, I want to cut her, too, out of my existence.

Oh, crap, I don't even know what I'm saying or doing or thinking.

Nothing in life makes sense anymore.

March 21, Thursday

6:31 p.m.

Just got back from rollerblading to the mall. But *everyplace* is soooo lonely. The strangest thing is that the more crowded places are, the more lonely they seem. I think I'm going crazy.

April 3, Wednesday

4:40 p.m.

I'm starting on my fourth month of being pregnant. It's like, UNREAL! I look in the mirror, and I don't even recognize my own body. It's like someone else's. Whose is it going to be next month, and the next and the next? I'm like, not a kid anymore, straight and strong and stringy. I'm . . . I'm too fat around the waist to button up my jeans or anything else tight. Guess from now on I'll just wear sloppy stuff. IT'S GROSS. I'M GROSS. LIFE IS GROSS.

What happened to the sunshine?

10:00 p.m.

Mom is worried about me. She's given up her whole life to take me to movies and shopping and to the lake, and everything else she can think of to keep me from becoming so depressed that I'll . . . I'll what? If *I* don't know *what*, how can she ever know *what*?

11:21 p.m.

I woke up from a crazy dream about having been
to a kegger. I was sitting by myself in a corner, but
I was so happy and content that *I wish I was doing
it*! No, I don't! I wouldn't do that to the little kid
growing inside me. (I decided she was a little girl
a long time ago.) Anyway, since I chose to keep her,
I am at least going to be good to her. I can't even
imagine letting her get drunk from the alcohol in
my bloodstream . . . if that's how it works.

April 4, Thursday

12:02 a.m.

I can't sleep. I just keep thinking about her. I think
I'll call her Dawn. Like the Dawn of a new day.
She'll be that for sure in my life.

I can feel Dawn cuddled up in the crook of my
arm, soft and warm and smelling like all the sweet-
ness that Mrs. Marsdon's baby smelled of. I remember the softness of that baby's skin. It was softer
than anything else soft in the world.

After Dawn comes I'll never be lonely or alone
again in my whole life. She'll love me and always
be there for me! Not like my kitten that grew up to
be a cat and then just kept running away until she
finally got run over. No, Dawn will be with me

twenty-four hours of every day and night. *I'll belong* to, and with, something again! She'll be my baby, my friend, my confidante. She'll fill up all the blank holes I now have in my life. Oh, I'm so, so, so glad I'm having her. She'll be my everything!

April 10, Wednesday

4:19 p.m.

I just got home from school, and I hate it so much I could die. It's dull and useless and hard. Each day gets longer, and more and more depressing. Actually I've become an inward hermit, in a forest of people, totally alone. I guess I'll wind up like my father and his mother. Maybe I should go join them in their lonely, big, old, scary, dark house in their big, old, scary, lonely, dark forest. I remember they used to always keep their blinds closed, even on the brightest of sunny days. I'm getting kind of like that. All the blinds on the inside of me seem to be forever stuck closed. It's dreary and dangerous inside me, and I HATE IT! HATE IT! HATE IT!!! I tried to force myself back to a few days ago when I was happy, but that now seems like a strange faraway never-never land of pretense!

5:29 p.m.

Mom came home today lighted up like a birthday cake. She dropped her things in the chair and pulled me down beside her. "I think I've found the answer to your social problems." She grinned.

Feeling mean-spirited, I shot back, "Now you're adding 'SOCIAL RETARD' to all my other obvious faults."

She looked like a small child who had been slapped, and I fell into her arms in an apologetic heap.

It's the first time we've physically connected in forever—I've been so paranoid and frustrated and mentally messed up.

We cried together, and it was like a cleansing thing, a gluing-back-together experience. I was happy because I've missed our togetherness.

Finally I said, "So, what's the magical solution to your crazy-mixed-up kid's problems!"

"Well." She seemed unsure. "There's a special school for the district's UNWED MOTHERS in the old Elm Street Elementary building."

She told me the big, old, stone main building had been condemned, but that the small frame building on the north side had been updated enough to make it into some usable classrooms.

We talked about it for a long time. Maybe it would be what I needed. I hope so!

April 13, Saturday

12:01 a.m.

I've been thinking about it and a school for *just* unwed mothers sounds scary and disgusting. A place for tramps and "hos" so they won't rub off on the nice kids at the regular schools. Yeah, the *nice* kids like Tina and Danny and his gang of budding perverts!

April 17, Wednesday

4:29 p.m.

Tomorrow at 8:15 I start the school for "Social Rejects."

Just between you and me, I wonder if for the last three months I've been mainly rejecting people, or if they've been rejecting me: knowingly, overtly, and sadistically, like I've thought they have. I really did think they were doing it because they were self-righteous and LOOKING DOWN ON ME, but to-day Jenny came and sat by me on the grass, where I always take my brown-paper sack lunch, and at first I didn't speak to her, and she didn't speak to me; then she started crying like her heart was breaking, and she said, "Oh, Annie, I've missed you so much. It's like you've cut me out of your life completely, and I don't know what I've done." She asked me why I wouldn't ever return her smiles or her "Hi's," and I guess I didn't even see them because I was busy looking at the floor, so people wouldn't see the SCARLET A like a neon sign on my shirt.

I told her I was sorry, and I just hadn't been feel-ing well.

She asked me if it was because I'd broken up with Danny, and I disintegrated into a flood of tears. I wanted to confide in her every detail of . . . of . . . every single thing, but the bell rang, and we both had to blow our noses and wipe our eyes and run back to class.

Jenny was going one way and I the other, but as she turned the corner by the statue, she turned and yelled, "Hope I see ya at soccer soon."

That really startled me because I'd thought my fat belly was totally the topic of everyone at school: students, teachers, principal, and janitorial staff. How self-centered could I have been? *They* had other things in their lives! I wasn't the focal point of the universe as I thought I'd been for almost four months! But even if they weren't laughing and jok-ing about my predicament, *I* was tearing *myself* down enough for all of us!

I phoned Jenny, and we talked for hours like we used to do in the olden days B.D., before Danny. I told her I was P.G., and she cried with me and said she still wanted it to be like it *used to be* between us.

Can't you just see fat, four-months-along me playing soccer? Ha . . . ha . . . ha . . . boo . . . hoo . . . hoo . . . hoo . . . hoo.

Probably I'll never play soccer again, and I LOVED IT SOOOO MUCH!

April 22, Monday

5:05 p.m.

Started the new school today. It was like moving to Uranus, seventh solar system from the sun. There are only nine girls, but they've been there awhile, so they've connected. ME! I was a foreign, frightening, new, grotesque subspecies that didn't fit in with any of them.

9:00 p.m.

It was Horrible! Miserable! Totally deflating!

I'm used to being in honor's classes and *this* is like kindergarten. I thought I'd tell Mom and Jenny how funny it was—but it isn't funny! It's sad, sad, SAD, and BAD! Any attempt at trying to put on the positive front that I'd thought I'd put on would be nothing but a big bald-faced lie.

One girl there is so fat, she looks like she's going to plop her baby out on the floor any minute, or maybe she's going to have a litter like animals do. Nothing would surprise me.

April 25, Thursday

5:23 p.m.

Third day at UWM School. It takes me forever to get to my new school on the bus. And yesterday I thought it was even more evil and ugly than the first day; then today I went in the girls' room and heard soft crying and sobbing in the next stall. I asked what was the matter, and a little voice said, "Nothing . . . I'm . . . I'm . . ." I could barely hear the last two words, ". . . just . . . dying."

Quickly I dashed into her stall and found her with her head almost in the toilet water, which was brownish-bluish green. "I'll get help," I said as I turned to go, but she reached out one weak little fist and clamped onto my shirt like it was some kind of life link. Maybe it was—because she had taken all the medicine she could find in her house, plus two packages of stuff she bought at a drugstore on the way to school.

"Don't leave me and please don't tell anybody," she whispered in a way so tortured, I had to promise I wouldn't. She assured me she'd thrown everything up.

After I'd washed her face with wet paper towels and straightened her hair with my brush, we walked out to a burned grass area by the rusty old metal fence, which surrounded us like we were in prison. She told me about herself. It's really a tragic story. Her parents don't get along very well, and there are five other kids so she, being the oldest, is sort of the second mother.

I think it was good for the little kid to unload. Actually, she's a year older than I am, but she's a spindly little girl who looks like she's all belly. And she's not very pretty; in fact, she's not pretty at all, so it's no wonder that she fell for the first guy who came along and gave her some attention. She was fifteen, and he was in his twenties, but she believed every word he said about them getting married as soon as he got a better job and stuff. I feel so protective of her. I'm much bigger than she, so I'm going to take her some of my clothes tomorrow. She's got her pants pinned in the front with a big piece of cloth that holds both sides together, and she's wearing one of her dad's shirts. He is obviously a *very* grease-monkey-type man. I'm not trying to be demeaning; I just mean there are big grease stains on his shirt, which *is* clean.

Tammy is one of the sweetest girls I've ever met. She reminds me a lot of Jenny (a sort of homely, underprivileged Jenny!) but honestly, I've never felt this way about anyone before: protective, championing, almost mothering. I know she was desperate when she took the pills, and she, *like me, wants* to be the best mother in the world. I worry a lot about her though; she looks so fragile and pale. Her baby looks like it's half as big as she is, and sometimes I don't know how she keeps from falling over frontward, but I guess that is because the rest of her body is basically all skin and bones.

I wonder what happens to all that skin that's holding that big blob of baby in, after the baby comes out? Does it just hang down to your knees forever, like a collapsed plastic grocery sack? Of course, I know better than that, but it still seems scary and morose.

We're supposed to have a counselor come in twice a week who will answer all our questions for us, but she has had the flu or something, so I haven't met her yet.

April 30, Tuesday

5:10 p.m.

I am soooooooooo sad. I don't know when I've ever felt so sorrowful. Today our teacher, Mrs. Milton, was called to the principal's office on the speaker, so she asked me if I'd help Tammy a little with her assignment while she was gone. When we moved closer together at the table, I was absolutely flabbergasted at Tammy's lack of knowledge. How could she *ever* be expected to write a report on an article when SHE LITERALLY *COULD NOT READ*? She had no inkling of how to SOUND OUT WORDS! How can she ever get a job, even at a fast food place, when she can't read the menu on the overhead board or the words on the cash register? I thought anyone, absolutely anyone could work at a fast food place.

10:15 p.m.

I've been wracking my brain trying to think of how I can help Tammy. I've got to help *her* because how can she help *her child* if she can't help herself? Maybe I'll ask Mrs. Milton what I can do.

May 1, Wednesday

1:49 a.m.

I woke up with this brilliant idea bouncing around in my head like a Fourth of July sparkler. And it *will work*! I know it will work because I talked with Mom about it! If Tammy comes to school an hour early in the morning and stays a half hour late, I can teach her with the very same sound cards Mom used when she taught me to read. They're still in Great-Great-Grandma Goldern's old TREASURE

TRUNK, which we keep at the foot of my bed. I can hardly keep from getting up and scrounging them out right now! But maybe I should wait and have Mom help me in the morning to find stuff that can help Tammy. I wonder if I can wait till morning? I guess I don't have much choice, do I?

6:21 p.m.

Mrs. Milton was sooooo nice and appreciative that I want to help Tammy. She's really a nice lady. She doesn't have enough time to do half the things expected of her.

May 9, Thursday

9:14 p.m.

I have never done anything more exhilarating and fulfilling than teaching Tammy to make sounds and words and sentences out of squiggly lines! She's like a caged bird learning for the first time to fly. And *we're* planning *her* forever future, which will be entirely different than she ever expected it would be.

At first I wanted her to go on to college, but Mom and I talked it over and decided that would be totally unrealistic with her dad just working part time in a U-Haul place, and her mom on food stamps and stuff. I asked Tammy if she thought her parents could read, and she was really embarrassed when she said, "Probably not," then decided maybe her dad might a little but didn't think her mom could, at least not much, because they never had any written stuff around, *ever*!

Can you imagine that? Not growing up with picture books and magazines and newspapers with the funny paper section, and letter blocks and *Sesame Street* and *Reading Rainbow*, and so on. Tammy said her mom only liked soap operas, so that's what the kids all watched.

That seems so sad and deprived, but I guess they just don't know any better. However, Tammy will! Mom said she could come to our house for the weekend, and she'd buy her a new outfit and have her hair cut and permed. Doesn't that make her the neatest mom in the world? All that for a girl she doesn't even know.

May 12, Sunday
Mother's Day

11:01 p.m.

Tammy said her folks didn't celebrate it, but we do, and we did! Mom and I stayed up after she'd taken Tammy home and laughed and giggled like two little teenyboppers. I told her that I'd always wanted to believe in Cinderella but had had a little reservation . . . BUT NO MORE. . . . After Tammy had had her hair styled and permed and was in her new pink outfit, she looked like another person! She positively did! She looked like a model on the cover of *Seventeen* magazine (that is, if someone had airbrushed the belly out). I couldn't believe my eyes. I still can't!

Mom said that much more than half of her transformation came from the inner beauty that she had never before known how to let out. I believe that's true. I absolutely one hundred percent do! How could I *not* believe it when I saw it with my own eyes?

May 13, Monday

2:14 a.m.

I just had another brilliant revelation! Tammy should go to beauty school. Having seen the miraculous transformation in herself, she should be all excited about the possibility of doing the same thing for others.

I wonder how much it costs to go to beauty school, and where she will get the money? Is it a possibility?

COME ON SELF, BE POSITIVE. WE'LL GET IT ONE WAY OR ANOTHER.

5:14 p.m.

I cannot believe how fast Tammy is learning. We went to the public library and took out a bunch of easy beginner books, and I'm so proud of her, I can hardly stand it because she's not only learning how to read herself, she's teaching her brothers and sisters *and her mother*!

Isn't that the most exciting thing you've ever heard? And my mom is a real jewel. Each day she gives me a package of cookies to take to school so Tammy can take them home for treats after their family reading lesson.

I've decided that after my baby is born I'm going to donate one night a week to the library illiteracy reading program. Mom's going to go with me, and I truly think it's about the most honorable thing in the world we could do for humanity. Imagine not being able to read a stop sign or a job application or a danger sign or a menu or . . . that to me would be the most suffocating, imprisoning feeling there could possibly be . . . whoa! If I'm so damn proud of my own smarts, how come they didn't save me from getting into *this* huge mess of trouble? Also, though I did take the chastity vow, how *important* to me was it if the first boy who came along could

talk me out of it? What a lost loser I am! Poor Mom
. . . poor, poor . . . lost . . . me.

Hey, snap out of it. You've got the greatest, most
supportive, loving, forever-there mom in the world,
and she and you are going to the market to stock
up on cookies and then to a movie. It's funny how
I never really appreciated being with her till I got
. . . you know. She still bugs the heck out of me
sometimes, but I'm sure I do the same to her, a
million times worse.

The counselor came in today and we had an hour
long therapy session. It was interesting, but I didn't
participate much because I have my mom to talk
to, and most of the girls don't have a very good
communication set-up with anybody except their
friends, who it seems are as dumb and unenligh-
tened as they are.

We had all learned the *mechanics* of sex in our
old school, but either we weren't listening, or it
didn't register, or we *weren't* taught the *PERSONAL
RESPONSIBILITY* PART! Such dumb, naive little
jerks! Every single one of us believing that "OUR
GUY" loved us and would always be there for us.
That is, everyone but Lolanita. She'd had lots of
boys and didn't believe that "one in the bunch was
worth the dynamite to blow him to hell." Everybody clapped and shouted when she said that, and
it might have seemed fun and funny to them, but
it seemed like the worst possible tragedy in the
whole world to me. Aren't *FATHERS* supposed to
have as much responsibility for raising a child as
mothers? It's going to become a more and more
scary world if *they* don't start making some
changes. Every mother in creation can't be like

mine, who is both a good mother and father figure. But what do I know about that? Maybe again it's about the old thing that "if you don't know what you're missing, you may not miss it that much."

Anyway, back to Lolanita. Her questions were only about how she could get on welfare and have her own apartment. Dr. Milshaw explained *that route* was becoming less and less easy. Afterwards Lolanita told us that lots of her friends and relatives were on "the system and had been back as far as she could remember."

It made my blood curdle. How could anyone *not want* to be independent? Responsible? A big lump formed in my throat. *What about me?* Mom had been saving for over a year so she could buy a new Datsun to replace ours, which has almost 90,000 miles on it. She'd have to spend the extra money on the baby. She didn't complain, but I know she hates putting around in the old thing.

Crap, sometimes life is crappy!

May 22, Wednesday

10:56 p.m.

I hate my shitty new school! Seven pregnant girls and two who have had their babies sprawling around moaning and groaning about how tough their lives are. All of them except Tammy and Marie and Marinda and me fantasizing about how someday they're going to be successful, wealthy doctors, scientists, lawyers, marine biologists, etc., yet I've never seen a single one of them take a book home on any subject, or for that matter even do any schoolwork they didn't absolutely have to do. They don't have a clue how much work and money those professions demand.

I'm so grateful for Tammy and Marie and Marinda. We're all scholastically working our rear ends off to get out of the horrible messes we've got ourselves into. AND WE WILL!

Marie wants to go to secretarial school, and her parents and grandparents are going to loan her the money, which she'll pay back when she gets a job, and Dr. Milshaw says there is a chance she can swing some kind of loan or scholarship for Tammy's beauty school. Isn't that amazing when just a few weeks ago she couldn't even read! A scholarship, wow! I do hope she gets it.

May 23, Thursday

5:20 p.m.

This afternoon I'm feeling top-heavy and depressed!

I'm working hard at trying to be positive, but I'm failing miserably, and *I feel miserable*! I'm getting so fat and repulsive, I'm unstable, and I don't feel or even look like myself anymore.

May 24, Friday

5:43 a.m.

The alarm clock just went off. I hated it because I'd been dreaming I was with Danny again, and it was sooooooo wonderful, I didn't want to *ever* wake up! He was being just the *GOOD THINGS* he really is. Oh! If that were truly so! Anyway, now I'm awake . . . and life, as it is, goes on, yuck!

9:19 p.m.

Went to my stupid doctor this afternoon. He says I'm losing weight and it isn't good for me or the baby. How can I be losing weight when I'm blowing up like a balloon?

May 27, Monday

10:46 p.m.

The counselor came in again today, but we didn't talk about *anything* I wanted to talk about. Now Beta has started harping about getting started on welfare and child support and an apartment of her own, so then *she* wouldn't have *anyone* telling her what to do including her mother. Daranela is still considering abortion, even though she is well past the point where the counselor says no reliable doctor would perform it. Birdie says she's had three abortions, and it's no big deal.

Geraldina says the guy who "fixed her up" is nineteen and already has five kids floating around that he knows of. She says he brags about it, actually seems proud of it, even though he doesn't support any of them. She says it's sort of like a macho thing for the guys in her area to have lots of kids by different girls. I think that's so disgusting and sad that it almost makes me ashamed to be a human being. And I thought *I* was dumb!

I don't think most of the girls even listen to the counselor's advice. They just turn her off. I'M LISTENING! And I wish I had heard all this stuff before I met Danny. I had no idea how many guys do the old broken "I love you" thing and the "If you *loved* me you would do it" bit. Then they feel absolutely no remorse at dumping the girl. Life sometimes isn't very pretty.

May 28, Tuesday

7:26 p.m.

It's amazing how we've segregated at school. All the kind of worldly girls in one group, and us naive dumbheads in another. They treat us like we're retards, and we treat them like they're . . . I don't know . . . maybe scary? I don't understand most of them and their attitudes. OR MINE! I'm *really* ashamed of myself because Tammy asked me to go to the mall with her after school, and I said I had to help my mom. That was a big fat lie. I just told her that because . . . because I'm *ashamed of her* and she's my best friend! I'm soooooo mortified, and yet that's the YUCK! way it is. Who so high and mighty do I think I am? I won't think about it. I can't!

I am sooo mixed up! I don't belong or fit in anywhere! Maybe going to the school for unwed mothers was a mistake. But how could it have been any better in my old school? I couldn't have stood that either!

May 29, Wednesday

8:42 p.m.

Today I walked through the park and became even lonelier and depressed than ever when I saw a couple of kids about my age ripping by on their rollerblades. I almost started crying. It was really a weird feeling because I wanted with all my heart to run on home and crawl into bed and cover my head up with a pillow, but I couldn't; something beyond my control forced me to stay there and watch all the kids my age doing all the things I should be doing. I could feel my heart being wrung out inside me as I daydreamed of myself playing soccer, riding my bike, rollerblading, and just "hanging" with my gang of goofy, prank-playing, nutso, no cares, no pressures, no regrets, no pain, normal fourteen-year-old kids.

May 30, Thursday

4:43 a.m.

I think I've cried all night, but it hasn't solved any of my problems or reduced any of the contempt I feel for myself! What a loser I am. Hey, buck up. All this negativity might be hard on the baby. *She* doesn't deserve to be raked around in my dark, yucky mudhole.

Okay, all my old friends, well most of them, at least individually, try to be nice and polite when we meet, *but* it would be obvious to even a fence pole that they aren't quite comfortable around me.

Come on, miserable, pessimistic, negative boob tube, *that's* probably because of *your* attitude, right?

Maybe, but the guys from the old days *do* seem to be embarrassed to admit that I even exist. And I'll *never* ever, *ever* be able to forget a couple of days ago when I was coming out of the market and a bunch of grade school boys started making remarks about my being pregnant and how I got that way. It made me so mad that if I'd been Jean-Claude Van Damme or Walker, I'd have splattered each of them all over the parking lot.

5:29 p.m.

Jenny called and asked me to come to her fifteenth birthday party. She said her mom would like to take Deanna and Molly and Kathy and me to see a funny play at the Civic Center, then out for ice cream and cake because her dad had just gotten home from the hospital. I hadn't even heard about his accident, but I was really sorry because he's a really nice father kind of man, and she's a really nice mother kind of mother.

I'm kind of scared. I hope it will be like the old times, but maybe now, in my condition, I'll have more in common with Jenny's *mother* than with her!

That's idiotic, stupid and pure, Annie, trying to beat up on myself even on the few occasions when it isn't deserved!

I'm *going to go*, and I'm *going to have fun*, and *I'm going to forget* I'm in any way different than they are! So there!

June 6, Thursday

10:31 p.m.

I've been reliving the olden days, and we really were a fun bunch: happy, lighthearted and thinking we could conquer the world. What I wouldn't give to go back there. No, no, no, no, no. Soon I'll feel my little bitty baby squirming around in my belly, and I wouldn't give her up for anything.

Well??????

June 7, Friday

I didn't go to Jenny's party because Mrs. Milton broke her wrist and asked me to, at the last minute, help with a parent function at school. I felt privileged and that it was also a "first things first" thing.

Another rabble dabble day with the counselor. Half the kids don't seem half as interested in learning how to care for a baby—its health needs, its food needs, its emotional needs, plus parenting and such—as they are interested in learning how they can gain their complete independence and *welfare*!

We "Wanna Be's" (that's what the others call us) really do *want to be* Good Girls. Okay, so we made some dumb decisions. They're not going to control our lives forever! The counselor is helping us see that. *She* had a baby when she was a teenager. Now she's a successful psychologist who donates two hours a week to the Unwed Mothers program, and we really appreciate her, at least the WB's do. She never makes it *sound easy* but she shows by her example that it is *possible*. For a long time I wouldn't allow myself to think it was and I was afraid I'd ruined my entire future.

1:32 a.m.

I'm beginning to think my pregnancy is going to last forever. The first couple of months it was the "throw-ups," which I thought was from some stomach flu virus I'd picked up. Now my breasts are beginning to blow up like balloons, and they're so hard and painful that sometimes when I automatically roll over on my stomach (because that was my favorite way to sleep before being P.G.), I wake up in extreme pain.

Also I've noticed that a lot of the kids in my old school who used to just whisper and giggle when they saw me at the mall and stuff are now obviously telling jokes.

That hurts. It hurts a lot. And sometimes *adults* are worse than the kids. I've had them pretend they didn't see me, or whisper to each other, like I can't sense that they're talking about me. *They* should know better, but apparently they don't, or they don't care or . . . Now I'm trying to blame my two-cent personal evaluation of myself on someone else. Stupid thinking right?

"Right."

Hey, where did you come from? I'm glad you're back. I really missed you and I didn't even know it till NOW! Tell me how much *you* think I'm worth.

"A million periwinkles and a sea shell."

Oh thank you, thank you, thank you, dear self, friend. I'd completely forgotten that day on the sand dune when I told Mom I had the most wonderful gift in the world for her, "A MILLION PERIWINKLES AND A SEA SHELL." I was very little then, and those things seemed far, far above the worth of anything else in the universe, or maybe in all of the galaxies combined.

"That was a nice day, wasn't it?"

Possibly one of the nicest in my whole lifetime, and I'm soooo glad you brought it up because sometimes, no—most of the time now, I'm rude and mean and disrespectful to Mom. I really can't understand why, except that maybe when I feel like I'm of no conceivable use to anyone on earth, and I'm treating myself with utter disregard and disrespect, I just automatically start treating her the same way. Could I possibly be trying to tear her down to my dark, gooey inner-world level?

"Possibly, but . . ."

BUT WHAT?

"Why don't you try going back to the old 'building-up' lifestyle instead of the 'tearing-down' one?"

I can do that! And I will! I'll try to be "patient and long-suffering" like Mom.

'Night.

I gotta get some ZZZZZ's because it's *tomorrow* already.

June 14, Friday

5:50 p.m.

School's going better, Mom and I are getting along better, and life generally is more upbeat. I guess that is because *you* convinced me to start looking at my glass as being half *full* instead of almost empty, and ya know, it's a strange thing, but since I've been looking for the sunshiney things, I'm seeing them everywhere. I wonder if I was just looking for the negatives whether I'd be over- *or under-whelmed* by them too? It's spooky how much control we have over our own lives, isn't it?

Mom's yelling that dinner is ready. It's her turn to cook, and believe me her meals are much better than mine.

June 17, Monday

7:10 p.m.

Wonderful news! Lolanita had her baby last night. A five-and-one-quarter-pound boy. Mrs. Milton said she had a pretty hard time, but that everything is all right now. She'll start bringing him to school in a couple of weeks. That will be fun, and it will be great for all of us to sort of practice on him, so our own little kids won't have to be guinea pigs to our dumbness.

It's pretty nightmarish *thinking* of going through the birthing thing ourselves. We've seen films and stuff about average births, but we've also seen movies and heard horror stories about how bad it sometimes gets! Agh!

11:21 p.m.

I'll be glad when my baby finally gets here. I'm tired of my feet and ankles swelling and feeling like an old lady with a backache and charley horses in my legs and, oh, yes, the kidney infections. Twice I've had them, and I've felt like I had to go to the bathroom every two minutes, then I couldn't go, then sometimes I'd almost wet my pants before I could get there. I suspect my little guppie-goldfish baby will be just as glad to get outside as I'll be glad to have her here.

And the "pelvic exam!" Even the idea of big old, old, old, fat Dr. . . . you know . . . it's like . . . like the very worst. But I haven't had to have them since forever!

June 18, Tuesday

3:16 a.m.

I tried my hardest not to wake up from my beautiful dream. I wanted it to go on forever, for it to be real! Oh, I'd like soooo much for it to be real. Me and Danny back together again, me skinny and shining and shimmering, and him crying and pleading at my feet until I finally believed him. I DO BELIEVE HIM! Believe that he has grown up and that he's suffered as much about this as I have. That he wants to start over again, and never, never be mean to me again, but just kind and thoughtful and generous. Ummmmmmmm, he's all the things *now* I ever wanted him to be.

Our delicious dream went on and on as he told me how he'd broken ties with all the verbally and physically abusive friends he'd had, and that now he's ready to settle down and be the good husband and father he should be and wants to be.

The dream was so real, I know it must be some kind of an omen! But I'm still going to think on it, trying to be rational till . . . tomorrow? No, *Thursday*! Then I'll do something about it.

4:02 a.m.

Shall I write him a note? Phone him? Send him a present? A telegram? Do it right away? Wait till after I've had the baby and I've exercised and dieted until my body is back to being even better than it was before? Maybe I'll just let this be my dream secret till then. In the meantime, baby and I will in detail make all the decisions for our forever lovely and love-filled fairytale future.

Often in the past few months, the fear and aloneness has hurt by far worse than real pain . . . but that is over! Now I have dreams of each of my *real* and *perfect* tomorrows piled up one on top of the other!

> *Sweet dreams of all the days to come*
> *With Danny and me, and our little one.*
> *Lives filled with joy and love and laughter*
> *And dreams and hopes of a great hereafter.*
> *How do I love thee?*
> *Let me count the ways*
> *Through the rest of my nights, and the rest of*
>   *my days.*
> *Good night*
>   *Sweet Prince.*
> *Love like ours has never been before*

Nor can there ever, ever be
A love like mine for you
A love like yours for me.

Sometimes I *wish*—I *know*—I *should* just *forget* him—but . . .

June 20, Thursday

9:48 p.m.

I can't believe how immature the kids in my class are, even though most of them are older than I am. They aren't listening to the difficult, confining, extremely expensive side of having a baby; they're just thinking about no longer having to go to school and having another little human person as a pet kitten, someone who will be forever little and cute and cuddly, someone who will always love them and make them feel important.

They were all getting "high," fantasizing about that pipe dream, when our counselor dropped the bombshell on them that the GOP, pushed by the Christian Coalition, is trying to pass a bill to deny cash payments to single teen mothers, thereby trying to discourage out-of-wedlock births.

I couldn't believe the anger that flared up. It was like most of the lazy, selfish girls *expected* the government, or the state or SOMEBODY, ANYBODY, to take care of them! No feelings of responsibility at all for taking care of themselves or the little innocent babies that they were carrying around in their bellies.

Tammy and Marie and I went out by the fence afterwards, in disgust. We *wanted* to go to school and get an education so we could support ourselves and our children. We *didn't want* charity. Even Tammy, who had been on welfare all her life, felt sick to her stomach. Reading was teaching her to become independent, and she was willing to fiercely fight for it. I was so proud of her, I felt like her mother!

In a way we feel sorry for the kids who don't understand the excitement and self-worth that independence brings. *But?* What if my mom wasn't willing, or couldn't *help me?* Maybe I'd have to be on welfare too! Ugg—scary thought, go away!

June 23, Sunday

11:09 p.m.

Tammy's mom just called to tell me she'd had a baby girl, six pounds, two ounces. She said everything had gone pretty well and that Tammy would be coming home in a few hours.

I'd heard somewhere that the county hospital didn't keep welfare cases very long, and I'm worried as anything about Tammy. We went to her house a few times to pick her up when she stayed over or Mom took us places, and . . . well, her house is dingy and dinky and . . . *dirty*, just plain dirty and unsanitary. Not the place for a brand-new baby!

I wonder if Mom would let Tammy and her baby come stay here? I guess that wouldn't be a good idea, and I'm sure Tammy's mom would be insulted. Oh dear, I really hope everything turns out all right for her, for them both!

June 26, Wednesday

8:45 p.m.

Mom took me over to see Tammy, and her baby isn't pink and sweet and everything I thought it would be at all. It's . . . little and boiled-lobster red and shrunken and wrinkled like an ugly, pickled little mutant something, and it had pooped in its diaper, and the mustard-looking stuff that smelled like a mixture of everything awful I'd ever smelled before in my life dripped out from around the sides of its diaper and onto its blanket and everything else. I wanted to turn and run, but Mom squeezed my hand and reminded me to give Tammy the basket of things we had brought her and her . . . Oh, dear God in Heaven, I pray my baby won't be so pathetic.

And I wish this dumb school didn't last *all* summer—but *it does*!!

June 29, Saturday

7:24 p.m.

Mom took me over to see Tammy again, and I'm amazed at how much better her baby looks. She's still not pretty in any sense of the word, but she's . . . a little more human-looking.

Mom stayed in the car because she had some papers to check, and Tammy's two little sisters, who share her bedroom, were out somewhere, so we could talk. Tammy told me that the doctor had had to pull the baby out of her with a huge pair of plier-type things called forceps, but that she'd had gas or something, so it didn't hurt that much at the time. The rest I didn't want to hear, but she told me anyway, and I'm trying to block it out because I don't want anything like that to happen to me, and if it does, I'm certainly not going to tell any of the other girls if I have a baby before they do.

I wish the whole birthing thing was over. It's sooooooo somehow unnatural . . . or something, but then again, I guess it isn't.

Anyway, Tammy's looking forward to coming back to school as soon as she can, and she promised she's going to read the whole pile of books I brought to her from the library, and she's going to write a very short outline about the plot of every book. I wish all of the girls in our school were like Tammy; in fact, I wish all of the girls in the world were sweet as she is. I hope we'll continue to be best friends for life! She and her homely little baby and me with my beautiful one.

That was a horrible thing to even think. I'd erase it except tonight I've been writing with a pen, so I'll scribble it out.

Oh, Lolanita never did come back to school. She just dropped out of everything after her baby came; even Dr. Milshaw doesn't know what happened to her. But that won't happen to Tammy. Not in a million-zillion years.

July 5, Friday

10:21 p.m.

Tammy and her baby came to school today for the first time. It's exciting and wonderful, and baby Janie Dee has become a precious, beautiful, fragile little doll! We're all fighting to hold her and rock her . . . but not to change her diapers, especially the stinkies.

It was really fun to help bathe baby J. D., but I had no idea how slippery and hard to hold she would be naked. It was like her unhinged little body was covered on the outside with slime, and her inside with strong little springs that shot out when you least expected it. I am soooo grateful I'm having this experience before I have my baby.

I can't believe how small Tammy is. She's just skin and bones. Mom said I could give her some of my B.B. (before baby) clothes, but they would look like tents on her. Not that I'm big—rather I wasn't B.B.—but she's hardly there at all.

Just between you and me, Daisy. I'm dying to know where all the stretched-out skin went after Tammy had the baby, but I don't dare ask her to let me see; wish I did! And those forceps things still spook me something terrible. Maybe I'll ask Dr. Milshaw about them and the episiotomy—ugg—ick . . .

July 7, Sunday

11:33 p.m.

I haven't been feeling really great the last few days. My back aches, and I feel like I've got a horrible, stuffed-up head cold, only it's all over my complete body. I'm trying not to be too bitchy about it because I've been putting pressure on Mom for too long as it is. I hope this is normal, if it's normal for normal to be this miserable.

July 8, Monday

8:21 p.m.

School is becoming very difficult. Tammy's baby cries all the time. I'm nervous and upset and about to blow my cool any second. I hope if I do, it won't be on Tammy or little innocent baby J. D. Yesterday I wanted to scream at *her* to SHUT UP, and that's not like me at all, but lately *I'm not* like me. I don't even know who I am. I'm cross and demanding and snappy, and I don't know how Mom or any of the others can stand me. I can't even stand myself.

Ohhhhh, for a good night's sleep, where I don't have to get up every ten minutes to go to the bathroom, and my back doesn't ache, and my boobs don't throb, and I don't get cramps in my legs, and I can get over my constant constipation. I hate it. I hate it. I hate it.

And I hate *me*!

I'll never be the same again! There is *no way* I ever could be!

"Perhaps . . ."

And *you* SHUT YOUR PAPER MOUTH and stay out of my life too, Daisy stick-your-nose-into-everything bitch.

1:22 a.m.

Dear Daisy, I've been crying for two hours and beating up on myself thinking I was not worth forgiving but you've *got to* forgive me and help me get myself back together. I can't have Mom dragging me off to the loony bin to get rid of the little creature that's taken over my life and so completely changed it that I . . . wish . . . she . . .

"Don't say it, Annie."

I won't, Daisy! I promise I *never, ever will*!

"You're a sweet, good girl, Annie."

I'm not! I'm a slut like people say behind my back. I'm a fourteen-year-old pregnant nothing, nobody slut, who would be better off if I'd never been born.

"NO, NO, NO, Annie."

Yes, yes, yes. And my back is aching so bad, it's like I'm being stretched on the racks in some ancient costume movie. I don't know how much more I can handle. I stand up, sit down, lie on the floor, nothing helps! Owww, I need my mama, like when I was little. She could kiss it better, make me well again. Ohhhhh, ouchhhhhhh, *I really can't stand it any more*!!!!!!!!! I think I'm inches away from death.

I must have passed out with the pain or something because it's morning, at least it's daytime and the sun is streaming in through my window. Maybe I just had a horrible nightmare.

9:20 p.m.

I'm feeling too punk to go to school, and tomorrow is my birthday. I don't even care. Birthdays aren't fun when you're not a little kid anymore, and I'm in no way a little kid anymore. I'm a big fat cow, and I'm only seven months pregnant. Oh yeah, I'm going to the doctor for another exam tomorrow. It's not exactly the birthday present of my dreams. Having him poke and prod and listen and feel, but at least it's just on the outside of me *now*!

July 12, Friday

1:31 p.m.

I'm soooooo glad I tucked you way, way under my mattress before Mom took me to the hospital, but I was lonely as anything there without *you*!

The whole production was scary and blurry with me in the backseat of the car moaning and groaning, sometimes screaming and cursing at Danny, while Mom drove so fast, there were cars honking on all sides of us.

When we got to the emergency room door, there were people waiting for us with a stretcher, because Mom had called on her cell phone while driving. It's a miracle we ever made it.

With me on a gurney, green gremlins raced through endless halls and up slower-than-molasses elevators. My pains cut way down about that time. I think maybe stark fear, at least temporarily, superseded the pain. Anyway, after eons I was in a room glistening with lights that had big metal halos around them, and somewhere along the way we'd lost Mom.

The last thing I remember before I conked out, probably from the shot someone had given me, was my calling helplessly, "Mama, Mama. I want my mama. I don't want this dumb baby; I want my mama." Slowly, that too faded away into a blur of numberless people crowding into the small room and desecrating my already desecrated body.

I tried to yell for dear Danny to come save us, but darkness pulled in on me.

July 26, Friday

2:16 p.m.

It's been two weeks since I had Mary Ann. Mom and I changed her name. She came two months early, and she's premature and sickly. Some nights she cries almost constantly. It seems impossible that such a shrill eardrum-shattering shriek could emit from her tiny, shriveled, uncoordinated body.

Having *her* isn't anything like I thought it would be. I honestly did think I was prepared for a baby, but I'm not. No way! If she's not eating, she's crying or pooping or wetting or having to be bathed or burped, or she's spitting up all over me, or having diarrhea.

It was great when we were in the hospital with the nurses taking care of her, and I was being treated like I was a princess or something, but at home . . . uggggg. I'm a twenty-four-hours-a-day slave to *her* whims. AND, truthfully she's not all that pretty, and she doesn't like to be cuddled like I'd dreamed about: an all-warm and soft and sweet-smelling nestler. NO! She stiffens out her arms and legs and . . . poops or does something else disgusting, and I wish . . . but it's a *lot too late* for that!

The days and nights are sooooooooooooooo long, I didn't know they could be so long. Mom says I can't even go for a walk and leave the kid because she might choke or some other stupid thing. I am sooooooooooooo bored and so about to go crazy!

Dr. Milshaw tried to tell us it would be like *this*, but of course know-it-all, conceited me, I thought she was just being an adult exaggerator, like most adults are.

July 27, Saturday

3:19 p.m.

I can't wait until Mary Ann and I can go back to school. Mom's real good about staying with her so I can see for myself that there is still some kind of life outside these restrictive walls, but I feel like a mutant type of organism, not at all like my old friends who haven't been through the P.G. thing, and not really comfortable at Tammy's house or Marie's house either.

Tammy's folks are nice people, but they're SCREAMERS, and they're *so* poor! It always makes me think that someday Mary Ann and I might be *there*. And Marie, she's still P.G. and . . . I dunno . . .

July 28, Sunday

sometime

My clock broke, so I not only don't know what time it is, I don't have any idea at all what date it is. I only know that I've been caged here for light years and centuries and millenniums.

The only reason I know it's Sunday is because Mom's home with Mary Ann, and as I was walking many, many, many blocks from our house, I heard church bells in the distance. I was drawn to them, and after a while I heard soft organ music. It was like I was hypnotized, and I zombied toward the sound.

The door was open, so I just walked in, sat down and appreciated *my* being able to do what *I* wanted for a change.

I stayed until the man quit practicing and picked up his music and left. Then it was cold and creaky and spooky in the old chapel. The thought passed through my mind that it would be a good murder mystery location. "Young unwed mother butchered in cathedral during Bach rehearsal." That sounded so realistic and possible that I got up quickly and left, not knowing where I was going from there, just knowing I didn't want to go home!

I'M NOT READY FOR ALL THE FRIGGING RE-SPONSIBILITY THAT'S ON ME THERE! I'M NOT SURE I EVER WILL BE, EVEN WHEN I'M TWENTY-NINE OR THIRTY-TWO OR ONE HUNDRED AND SEVEN!

July 29, Monday

2:29 p.m.

Mom bought me a new clock, so at least I know what time it is. I wish I didn't! I'm every day hating time more. Mary Ann is gaining weight fast, and pretty soon, I hope, I hope, I hope!—we'll be on the bus for school. She and Tammy's baby, J. D., can sleep in the nursery there while we try to not only catch up in school but to accelerate. We both are driven to get ahead and make something of ourselves, so we can care for our kids. Marie is not quite as ambitious, but she certainly isn't like the others who are totally takers and users; some of them even wanted . . . but I don't need, or even want to think about that.

July 30, Tuesday

8:30 p.m.

Mom came home late, looking pale and tired. I was ashamed I hadn't fixed us something to eat. I could have done that! But no, *I'm* too busy groveling in my "poor me" state. Mom said she'd been out on a few interviews for a night or weekend job.

"You can't do that," I said selfishly. "I can't take care of Mary Ann *all* the time *all* by myself."

Mom looked completely beat and told me she was doing everything she possibly could to be supportive of us, but that she'd found her insurance didn't cover as much as she'd hoped it would and . . . she held out her hands in despair.

I broke up and started telling her how I *knew*

Danny had changed, and that he and his rich father would *want* to help us, and that perhaps Danny and I would even . . .

Mom waited for a minute or two, then quietly said that she'd talked to both of them shortly after she'd found out that I was pregnant, and not only had Danny denied being Mary Ann's father, the two of them threatened to ruin my reputation completely if I even considered DNA testing. Danny said the whole football team would swear they were all . . . using me . . . and knowing *they* probably would lie for him, I started pulling into myself like a turtle pulling into its shell. I wanted to just totally disappear forever, but Mom wouldn't let me.

This has been a bad night, but it's been a good night too because Mom and I just sat and talked and hugged and cried together for a long time, then Mary Ann started fussing but not really crying, so I went and got her and nursed her while Mom and I hugged and cried some more. After Mary Ann had finished eating, she just cuddled up like I'd always dreamed she would, and the three of us nestled together in a soft, quiet, loving little love ball. I mentioned Dad helping, but Mom said he and Grandma lived on her pension and social security in their old, run-down rural house.

It's strange, but I'll never forget this beautiful, hurtful night! It's emblazoned in my mind in red neon! It's in a way kind of like I'm going to get well now.

While Mom took her shower, I made us some soup and a salad, with the baby lying in the middle of the table. She literally was the centerpiece of both the table and my life. I'd never felt such love for her. She lay there making strange melodic *beyond* melody sounds that were more spiritual than anything I had ever heard, even the Mormon Tabernacle Choir singing the "Battle Hymn of the Republic," and suddenly I realized that I COULD MAKE IT! I COULD GO ON FROM HERE AND BE ALL THE THINGS I'D EVER WANTED TO BE AND MORE! What an exhilarating feeling! I wish I could make it last forever!

July 31, Wednesday

5:10 p.m.

The parcel post man just delivered a big box from Dad. He writes a note or phones for three minutes a couple of times a year, but . . . he's really almost a stranger to me. Maybe I should say he *was* almost a stranger to me, but no more. HE'S SAVED NOT ONLY MY LIFE BUT MY SANITY with the adorable pink-flowered stroller he sent to: "My little Annie's L'il ANNIE."

I wish it weren't so cloudy and semi-windy and I could take L'il Annie out for a ride, right now! Ummmm, I guess we can wait though till tomorrow, but for now I'm going to take her for a stroll around our apartment and possibly even down through the halls.

10:12 p.m.

I hate like everything Mom having to take a job as a waitress with her having a master's degree and teaching credential and everything, but she's really emphatic about it. She says she can make two to three, maybe even four as much being a waitress in the prestigious Peach Tree Hotel as she could make any other place. Which will mean less time there and more time with me and Mary Ann.

I didn't realize I was such a snob. I'm truly ashamed . . . still . . .

12:47 p.m.

Mom just got in. She worked a big formal dinner party Mr. Goldmeyer was giving for his wife. It was their fiftieth wedding anniversary, and he'd bought her a magnificent diamond bracelet, which he'd put in her soup. Somehow *it* had gotten mixed up with the other bowls, and he was furious until Mom found the bracelet and, in her quiet, easy way, handed it to him, then distracted Mrs. Goldmeyer, so he could slip it into *her* soup bowl.

He was so delighted with Mom's cool efficiency

that later he slipped two tightly folded one hundred dollar bills in her hand. Imagine $200, plus her part of the fifteen percent tip and her regular wage.

We laughed about her giving up her teaching job altogether, but, of course, we know she won't because she feels TEACHING is one of the most honorable and important needs in the world! I tend to agree with her, and I've slightly considered that . . . but I would like to go into one of the megabucks professions too. We'll see. I guess I've got a few good years left in me since I only turned fifteen a few weeks ago.

August 2, Friday

12:00 Noon

I'm having home school since Baby Annie isn't big enough to go with me to Unwed Mothers school. My teacher, Mrs. Darnell, had a stroke and is partially paralyzed on her right side, but she's kind and gentle and *very* intelligent. She expects a lot of me because she says I "have a great deal to offer." *That's* good for my ego! She's always telling me to "stretch my mind," that I "have no idea how far it can go till I try it." Isn't that a stimulating thought?

Life isn't quite so bad now that Mrs. Darnell comes twice a week, and I take Baby Annie out walking nearly every morning and afternoon, but I'm still sooooooooooooooooooo lonely! I seem to be neither fish nor fowl.

Yesterday we were in the park, me sitting on a bench like I was one of the old men or ladies feeding the pigeons, when a couple of kids from my old school bicycled by screaming and laughing, and I felt like another species on the food chain, probably the lowest, most insignificant one, because they passed me like I was invisible.

I wanted so much to be one with them that I had a single wild moment of wanting to stash Baby Annie in the bushes and take out after them, happily yelling and screaming myself. Of course, I didn't. I couldn't. But I still *wanted to* with some kind of an inner aching and emptiness that is impossible to put into words. Actually, words aren't nearly wet enough!!!!!!! I know that doesn't make sense, but it's exactly how I feel. I wonder if in my whole lifetime I'll ever be all put back together again?

2:30 p.m.

I met old Mrs. Abbot in the apartment house hallway, and she played with the baby for a few minutes, then told me that if I ever wanted her to tend, she would love to. I was so delighted, I almost jumped out of my shoes. She's going to do it this afternoon, and imagine . . . I'LL BE FREE, FREE, FREE for at least a while.

I think I'll get my rollerblades out and see if I still remember how to keep myself upright. It has been so long since I've been JUST ME and doing JUST ME THINGS!

WOWIE . . .

ZOWIE . . .

POWIE! I can hardly wait.

August 3, Saturday

4:42 p.m.

I've never had so much fun in my life. I bladed to the park and found some kids playing street hockey. They let me join, and I can't believe how good I was, or . . . maybe how bad they were. Anyway, it was a blast from the past. I absolutely cannot wait to do it again.

See ya.

Gotta go pick up the baby.

August 4, Sunday

10:37 p.m.

Today when the baby and I came in from our walk, we found Mom sitting upright in a kitchen chair, sound asleep. I didn't know people could do that, and I thought at first she was dead. Obviously, she'd come in from school and dropped her stuff on the table and leaned back in the straight chair and just conked out. It was scary and bizarre because her eyes were half open.

Crazy thoughts scrambled around in my head, like maybe she's had a stroke . . . then what would happen to us? *That* might be *even worse* than if she was dead because then I'd have to take care of Mary Ann and her too. But that was dumb, nothing could be worse than having her dead.

Well, anyway she was just exhausted.

I've been trying not to think about it, but I know she works too hard, and we simply can't let anything happen to her.

I'm sooooo sorry and ashamed that Baby Annie and I are such a burden to her, but I haven't a clue as to what I can, or should, do about it.

Oh CRAP, CRAP, CRAP. What a miserable excuse for a daughter I am. How could I ever have done this to her?

August 7, Wednesday

1:49 p.m.

Stupid me! I thought I had this brilliant idea that turned out to be about as worthless and useless as most of the other things I think about or try. Actually, it seemed good in the beginning when I thought I'd go out and get an evening job, so I could still go to school and stuff. I was sure Mrs. Abbot would take care of Baby Annie two or three nights a week, and I'd be able to take some of the load off Mom.

So, what happened? you ask.

Well, first of all I got out the résumé that I'd helped Mom write when she first decided to get a second job. I thought I could make mine sort of like hers. WRONG! She had a list of things she'd done and people to call as references. I had nothing! Nada! ZIP!

Still I forced myself to fill out applications at McDonald's, Wendy's, Chuck A-Rama, Sizzler, Brick Oven, The Dollar Store, and three flower nurseries. *None* of them could use me even when they had HELP WANTED signs in their windows. Finally I asked the man at Hip Hops, *why*? And he said because I was "too young to hold a job."

Yeah! Barely fifteen. Too young to hold a job! Too young to drive a car! Too young to drink or smoke! Too young to quit school! Too young to date—but *not* too young *to have a baby* with all the expenses and physical and mental horrendous responsibilities that go with it! LIFE DOESN'T MAKE *ANY* SENSE AT ALL! Hey! *Whose* fault is all this?

August 8, Thursday

1:15 p.m.

Mrs. Abbot tending the baby occasionally is saving my sanity, and, thank goodness, she won't let me pay her—as though I could! The doctor said Mary Ann and I can go back to school in another week. Until then I'm floating on a shaky quicksand field. Nothing seems quite real anymore.

6:45 p.m.

Listen to this, Miss Nosey Daisy Diary.

I met Will Peters when I was out riding my bike. He was riding his, and we raced up the bike trail to the top. We used to go to my old school together, although I was in seventh grade and he was in the ninth, but it was like nothing had happened in between. We laughed and joked, and he said I was the fastest and best girl rider he'd ever seen. On the way back we stopped at Jelly's to get a coke and he asked me if I'd like to go out Friday night.

I almost fell off my chair, I was so surprised and delighted. Did I want to go? Do kids like candy?

Do you think I should go? He probably knows all about me and Danny and . . . *so*! I'm still me!

I wonder if I should go. It could be awkward, like if he asks what I've been doing or something, what would I say?

But it *wasn't* awkward today. It was nice and I WANT TO GO WITH HIM. ACTUALLY, I WANT TO GO ANYWHERE WITH ANYBODY! No, I'm not really that desperate, but I've got to start having a life again sometime.

August 10, Saturday

12:44 p.m.

I can't believe such *awful things* can happen to me! Somehow I seem to be like a magnet for pain and disrespect and ridicule and everything else that is negative and sordid.

Will kept saying over and over that I asked for it. But I didn't. Believe me, Daisy. I really, truly didn't! I honestly thought that he was just asking me out like normal guys ask normal girls out, but . . . well, back to the beginning.

Mom was working a big convention party, and Mrs. Abbot was going to baby-sit, so I felt like Miss Junie Prom on her first date. Well, not really a *date* because Mom doesn't believe in "dating" till a kid is sixteen. *That* is ironic, isn't it? Mom not wanting me to "really date" until I'm sixteen, and I'm barely fifteen, and I've already had a baby!

So, of course, I had to lie about things as usual and say I was going out with Tammy and Marie to a movie, and that Marie's mom was going to take us.

I know this makes me sound like a horrible person and all like that, and I really don't want to be like that, but I did think it was just going to be a bunch of kids hanging out and goofin' off and . . . actually, *I guess I didn't think!* I just wanted to do something fun. But it wasn't fun at all; it was just another "kegger." The kids were all slopped within the first half hour and had turned their brains off and their hormones and animal instincts on!

A couple of guys were hammering out what I guess they thought was guitar music, but it was just ear-splitting noise. I was disgusted and repelled, and I told Will I wanted to go home. He just laughed and said there was no way he was going to let me "ruin the party." Then he said it was a little late for me to start playing "Polly Pure," and he started getting grabby. It made me so mad that I picked up a big stick and I was about ready to—I don't know what—when a guy I didn't even know offered to drive me home. He seemed nice and quiet and shy, but I had him let me off three blocks from my house anyway and gave him a wrong telephone number.

I feel like such a lost cause! Will I ever meet a nice guy? Are there any? I think I'm going to become a total recluse like my dad and his mother, then I can't be hurt any more. I wonder if that's why they like living alone in such a lonely place? If that is the reason, at this moment, it seems like a good, valid one, but . . . I don't think it would be a good way to bring up a child, do you?

I've always dreamed of getting married. Now, I don't know?

August 15, Thursday

6:59 p.m.

Mary Ann and I started real school again today. It was sooooooooo wonderful! Tammy's baby and mine were in the nursery, just off our school room, and I guess it is about as good as things can get under the circumstances. It's weird though how Tammy and I both used to like to practice on other babies, but *we* don't want anyone to touch ours! It's okay for them to watch us bathe our babies and things like that, but . . . I guess we're overly protective. If so, that's the way it is, and that's the way it's going to stay!

Tammy and I are both working hard at acceleration, and Mrs. Milton is helping us. She thinks I can graduate high school when I'm seventeen if I go to summer school, and Tammy can pass her high school equivalency early, then she can go on to beauty school, and I can go to college. I'm still not sure if I want to be a teacher or a counselor, but I guess I've got lots of time to figure that one out. I'd still love to be a pediatrician if it didn't take so dang long.

. . . or a writer . . . I don't know.

9:46 p.m.

It's pretty exhausting getting up and feeding and getting L'il Annie and myself ready for school, then toting her stroller and stuff and my books and stuff onto the bus, then to the corner closest to our school and walking four blocks.

After school, traipsing all the junk home, straightening the house, and helping with dinner and washing and . . . it never ends . . . It *never, never* ends, *and* there is never, *never, ever* any time for *me!* It's like I'm in a time warp in cyber space or something . . . so tired, so all the time, every pore of my body tired, tired, worn out and tired to the bone-weary.

Whatever made me think that me . . . just a dumb, dumb, dumber-than-dumb kid myself could . . . FOR *TWENTY-FOUR HOURS OF EVERY! EVERY! EVERY! EVERY NANO-SECOND AND MINUTE OF EVERY SINGLE SOLITARY DAY FOR THE REST OF MY KID LIFE* HANDLE ALL THE PUKING AND POOPING AND SCOPING AND WETTING AND SCREAMING AND BAWLING AND BATHING AND WASHING AND CLEANING AND FEEDING AND HOLDING AND ROCKING AND WALKING . . . I'm not *me* anymore, I'm just . . . it's like *she* grew inside of me like a cancer or something that *was* a part of me— now . . . It's like science fiction, *I'm a part of it* . . . her . . . the thing . . . I'm not me!!!!! I'm . . . I don't know what I am, BUT I WANT TO BE JUST *ME* AGAIN.

I wish with all my heart, I truly do, that I'd never met Danny, and most of all I wish . . .

I wish I had never gotten pregnant . . .

    I

        wish

            both me and Danny

                were

                    dead. DEAD! DEAD! DEAD! DEAD!

                    DEAD!!!!

ACTUALLY, ALL THREE OF US—

   DEAD

           DEAD, DEAD, DEAD, DEAD.

             MORE THAN DEAD!

August 16, Friday

5:10 a.m.

I can't believe what I wrote last night, but sometimes I feel so blue and beat that maybe it's good to get rid of it any way I can.

BUT I don't really wish that Baby Mary Ann and I were both dead. . . . Danny? . . . maybe . . . maybe not. I still hope that . . . but maybe I shouldn't do that either. *Wishful thinking doesn't make things so!*

11:21 p.m.

I'd *really* like to be young again! Playing stickball on Carter's dead-end street; boys and girls just being kids instead of . . . I don't know . . . *boys* and *girls* . . . life was so much easier when we were all sort of nonsexed: climbing trees, riding bikes, skating, playing soccer. I wish I could go back to that happy never-never land, that maybe *never-never was*.

August 17, Saturday

1:17 a.m.

I can't get out of this nightmarish, horrible existence I've been in the last week or so. There is absolutely no *color* in my life, no color, no music, no light, no joy. I've been trying to figure out how those words can *just be words* with no meaning . . . no anything . . . anymore.

I don't want to be like this. I want to *get out* of my black funk, but it's like I'm trapped inside an oil barrel, and it's too slippery to make any headway out even if I tried, which actually doesn't seem worth the effort.

I do all, well most, well, maybe just the things I absolutely have to do to get by. Mom nags, and the kid cries, but neither one of them can possibly imagine what I'm going through, the energy it's taking just to exist.

School is a bore, and I have absolutely no appetite; in fact, food tastes like cardboard. I thought maybe I should go to the doctor, but what would he say? Probably that I have a bad attitude, and I need to pull myself together and start *MAKING* myself happy, and all the other trash words that don't compute in my thinking anymore.

I think I'll ask Mrs. Abbot if she can take L'il Annie for a while tomorrow, so I can maybe go to a movie or something to get away . . . mainly get away from myself! That doesn't make any sense at all, does it? But I guess that's the mode I'm in right now.

Each day I feel more depressed, confused, and overwhelmed. I feel that each nano-second, I'm becoming more and more sucked under by the black what-ever-it-is that is taking over my world.

Mom has a new second/extra job in charge of conventions and large parties. She's never home on weekends. Mrs. Abbot has gone to her daughter's for two weeks. Tammy and Marie live too far away for me to go see them. So! *I'm* being literally suffocated and strangled by my own (probably self-induced) depression.

I've missed school a lot, and Mom isn't even aware of it. I told my teacher L'il Annie is sick.

Thank goodness she's a good baby because I feed her and bathe her and change her and *that's all*!

I've become a rotten, inattentive, uncaring, unfeeling person. *THAT'S IT! THAT'S WHAT'S HAPPENED TO ME!* I can't feel anything anymore! I *can't care* one smidge about any other smidge!

I've got to *do* something! But what? Maybe if we just went to the mall. It used to be exciting.

3:21 a.m.

Oh dear, dear, dear Daisy:

I am sooooooooooooooo scared. I know I must be some sort of crazy, multipersonalities person or schizophrenic or . . . or . . . I don't know what, but something . . . maybe just evil and selfish, but anyway I'm certainly not the nice good-judgement person I used to be I . . . I . . . I *must* tell you about it. But *please, please* don't hate me, unless you absolutely have to!

I'm soooooo mortally self-wounded and humiliated and degraded, I don't know if throughout my life I can ever live it down. But . . . it seemed so rational at the time. I know this won't make one iota of sense to you, but I'm honestly going to tell it to you like it actually happened.

About 4:30 I knew I had to get out of the apartment or explode in one wimpy little whimpering mess. I remember my hands shaking as I dressed L'il Annie in the new pink dress Mom had bought her and put the little pink ribbon around her head. I wanted her to look nice, even though I was perfectly satisfied with myself looking like a laundry bag full of wet wash.

When we got to the mall I saw Deanna and Kathy and Meg ooing and awwing in the Gap window and pushing each other around like happy, babyish, no-problem, no-pressure, no-cares kids.

I haven't any idea what happened to me at that point; I only know some compelling sort of inner energy wanted like everything to go push their silly, scatterbrained, empty heads right through the glass. It was sooooooooooooooooooooooooooooooooooooo morbid and so scary! I wondered what had happened to me to change me from a happy earthling like them to the desperate, degenerate . . . whatever I was.

Mary Ann chose that very moment to "pooh" in her diaper with a loud rumbling and a stench that permeated the whole mall. She must have had some gas too because she started bawling like *I* was physically abusing her in some horrible way.

I could feel everybody staring at us in disgust, so I quickly started pushing her toward the ladies' room as fast as I could.

I got some wet towels and started to change her, then realized I hadn't brought any extra diapers. It was a nightmare. Two girls came in, looking at us like they were going to throw up, and immediately turned and dashed out. I wanted to slump down in the corner with my arms over my head, and I probably would have done that if I'd been home. But in the mall, I had to try to just wrap Baby Annie's bare bottom in her blanket.

She screamed and kicked and turned red and "poohed" some more. *It* was all over, and I begged her to be still so I could semi-clean her up, but she wouldn't! She just kept yelling louder and harder and redder and "poohing" more and kicking more, until I TOTALLY LOST IT.

I AM *SOOOOO* ASHAMED, DAISY! WILL SHE EVER BE ABLE TO FORGIVE ME? WILL YOU?

WILL I BE ABLE TO FORGIVE MYSELF? WOULD MOM IF SHE EVER FOUND OUT ABOUT IT? OH, I HOPE SHE DOESN'T! *I'M SURE* SHE COULDN'T FORGIVE ME, WORLDS WITHOUT ENDS!!!!!!!!!!!!

How could I ever have had *even* a fleeting desire to put Baby Annie's blanket over her head and suffocate her? Would I actually have done it if the elderly woman hadn't hobbled in? I remember after she left, I took a deep, frightened breath, looked at myself in the mirror and . . . you know what? . . . I could *NOT* IN ANY WAY RECOGNIZE THE WHITE, BLANK-FACED GHOUL THAT STARED BACK AT ME.

I need help bad, Daisy!! I really truly do!!! But back to the mall . . . as I was coming out of the ladies' room, I felt a soft, filmy, comfortable whiteness encompassingly float over me, and immediately suspected that I was starting to faint, so I hurried for the nearest bench.

I sat on it in the middle of the mall by the fountain for I have no idea how long. People passed, some stopped and looked at my now sleeping baby and said how pretty she was; one or two asked if I was her big sister or a sitter. That hurt. It hurt a lot, for me and for Baby Annie too! Every child deserves to be raised by a *MOM*, not a dumb, stupid kid that doesn't know from up.

That experience was so overwhelming that later, when I saw a young married couple come out of a store, arm in arm, and looking like they owned the world, I wanted them to have L'il Annie.

The idea passed as quickly as it came, but in a few minutes, a scared and lost little child came out of one of the stores and immediately the lady was there to kneel beside him and take his hand in hers. I couldn't hear what she was saying, but I knew in my heart it was about them maturely taking good care of him until they found his mature mother.

Each day I'm going more crazy. I can't understand why Mom can't see it! *I can see it* when I look in the mirror, and it's horrifying. My eyes are stoned and glassy-looking, and I haven't washed my hair in I-don't-know-when, and I don't care about it, or anything else. Even the baby is suffering. Often I can't remember to even feed or change her till she cries.

When Dr. Milshaw called last week, I told her I was having home school. She bought it! *WHY* didn't she understand and come to my rescue? Why doesn't somebody? Anybody? Why don't they care?

That's not fair. I know Mom *cares*, but she shows me the stacked up hospital bills for me and for the baby (that her insurance doesn't cover) and diapers and baby food and stuff. I can't believe how much they cost! No wonder so many of the kids at UWMS (Unwed Mothers School) try so hard to get on welfare. I wish *we could* because now I feel that neither me nor Baby Annie has a mother. But my mom wouldn't do that; she's too proud and honorable. I guess I am too, rather, I *used to be*. Now I want, I need, I've *got to have* a mom, even if it's a "stay-at-home welfare mom." Or do I? I don't know what I want, except maybe just to go to sleep and never, never, ever wake up.

August 18, Sunday

11:42 p.m.

Last night Mom got in after I'd gone to bed. As she kissed me good night and tucked me in, she told me she thought I looked pale, that maybe I should get out in the sunshine more and take better care of my body. If she only knew what was happening *in my head*!

Well, I took her advice, and this morning I fixed myself a lunch and a jar of baby food and a couple of bottles. I could only nurse L'il Annie for a week or so (and then naturally something went wrong in that area too). BUT this time I remembered diapers, lots and lots of diapers because I thought we'd probably be gone for most of the day.

I'd read in the paper that a big gourmet grocery store and strip mall were opening up on the other side of town. The superexpensive side.

There was a miniature park thing by the side of a precious baby store, and I peeked in at some of the things as I passed, but I knew they'd be far, far more expensive than we could afford. In fact the one little white dress with bitty seed pearls on it and one tiny, teeny pink rosebud by the waist had a ticket that hadn't been completely turned over.

Its price was $89.50. Imagine over $90 with tax, for a baby dress that L'il Annie would wear maybe half a dozen times.

Still, I couldn't get my eyes off the dress. Annie would look adorable in it. She needed it. She deserved it! Why shouldn't she have it?

As I began to almost obsess on the dress, *guess what*? The same beautifully dressed, gorgeous lady who had found the little lost boy in the mall stopped to look in the toy window next to the baby shop. I thought I saw longing and baby-hunger in her eyes, and before I really knew what I was doing, I pushed Mary Ann's stroller where she couldn't miss it and ran to hide behind a bush and wait and watch. When she got close, and I saw the delighted smile on her face, mixed with one of caring alarm, I took off around the corner and ran down the street as fast as I could.

After sprinting three blocks, I was stopped by my own blood sloshing up in my ears *AND* the horrifying thought . . . What if the loving young couple didn't want to take Annie? What if a pedophile found her first? What if he used her for baby kiddyporn movies?

By the time I got back to the place where I'd left L'il Annie, I was completely red-faced and out of breath. In fact, when I couldn't see her stroller around, I literally became sick to my stomach. Hysterically, I started calling, "Where is she? Where is she? Where is she? Who took my baby? Who's kidnaped my baby?"

People started coming out of stores all around the area. Most of them pulled away from me almost in fear, but I couldn't stop yelling. It was like an automatic reflex or something.

Finally, after a forever of forevers, two uniformed policemen came. Each took me by one arm and led me away. "Shhh, girl, you're causing a commotion, so just settle down." One of them said as he grabbed a tighter hold on my arm, "We're taking you up to security where we'll get this thing straightened out if you'll cooperate."

It wasn't till then that I realized I'd been struggling and continuing to yell.

"I just want my baby. I just want to know she's all right," I blubbered, tears splashing down my face until I could hardly see.

They took me up some dark stairs and down a long, dingy hall. "Sorry we couldn't take you on the elevator, but you were making too much fuss," one of them said almost in a fatherly manner, as he tried to guide me and talk on his cell phone at the same time: just a bunch of garbled words and numbers.

They led me into a room so small that the five of us there were almost sitting on each other's laps. Slowly, as though they had all the time in the world, and Baby Mary Ann had no importance at all, they began interrogating me endlessly: What was my name? Address? Phone number? Mother's name? Where did she work? How could they contact her? Where was my father? Where did he live? How could they contact him?

They went on and on, often talking to each other as though I weren't even there, until at last I couldn't stand it another second, and I stood up and screamed, "None of the stupid crap you stupid cops are asking is important at all! Where's my baby?"

I realized what a horrible, terrible, stupid, miserable, low-class mistake I'd made. Now they'd think, probably know, that I *wasn't fit* to have my baby, *any* baby around me. For a few seconds my heart felt like it had stopped beating as I tried to explain how shatteringly worried I was.

"Then why did you abandon your baby in a strange place?" one of the men asked coldly.

"I didn't abandon her," I whimpered. "I . . ."

"You what?" His words had icicles dangling from them.

"I . . . I . . ." I was so upset, I vomited all over his shoes and up one of his pant legs. As I continued to try to explain, I threw up again, but by this time everybody had backed away.

Between blowing my nose and wiping the tears off my face and the puke off my mouth, I tried to make up a story that might help get Mary Ann back. "I was just sitting there when I got so sick, I tried to run behind the little hedge thing to throw up."

They looked at me suspiciously, which made my shaking and twitching become so totally uncontrolled that I *knew* I was going to have a seizure-fit of some sort—until a big, old, black lie started creeping disgustingly out of my mouth. "I . . . I, well, after I'd thrown up until I felt I had absolutely nothing, nothing, nothing left in me: no partially digested, soured baloney sandwich or green, pukey apple or fermented, curdled milk or acid . . ."

The biggest policeman started turning green. "Okay, okay . . ."

I hesitated for a second, then forced myself to continue, knowing this might be the moment when I'd either lose or keep Mary Ann. "Then my diarrhea started, and I simply had to make a dash for the ladies' room. I thought it would just take a minute, but it didn't. . . ."

The five vultures were still staring down at me, repelled, but I could tell, not quite sold.

So I continued, "I dumped and I dumped and I dumped . . . sometimes throwing up . . . sometimes the other . . . in one way, it seemed like I wasn't in there very long; in another way, it seemed like forever. I wanted to leave. Honest, I really wanted to leave. But just imagine yourself in my position."

I could see the looks on their faces turn from revulsion to compassion. One even put out his hand and touched my shoulder.

I hated like everything that I had had to lie to them . . . but I wanted Mary Ann back at any cost, and I knew she was close because I could hear her sometimes making *her* special noises down some distant, hollow hall.

Isn't it funny how I could know my baby's sound from any other baby's sound in the whole wide world?

After a bit, they believed me and went and got L'il Annie. I think she was as happy to see me as I was to see her.

What if? But I can't think of *"what if's."* I can only think of L'il Baby Annie in her pink nesting corner of our room and that "God's in his heaven and all is right with the world." I can't remember who said that, but I'm going to look it up tomorrow.

Anyway, the policemen brought us home in a

squad car and told me what a lucky girl I was to still have my baby.

They didn't say anything about calling Mom, so I guess I'll just keep my fingers crossed. I do hope they don't have to contact her because . . . because . . . I couldn't go through all the terrible truth and the even more terrible lies and stuff again.

August 19, Monday

5:15 a.m.

Dearest, dearest friend, Daisy Diary:

My heart is breaking because I've definitely decided that I must do what I have to do! I've confided so many awful, terrible things to you that Mom could never ever love me completely again or respect and trust me *at all* again if she knew. SO, the only solution is to, Friday, before the trash man comes, cut you up in little bits and put you in the bin.

I'm sorry Daisy, but there seems to be no other way. I'm probably too old for a diary now anyway; at least being a mother and all should make me more mature. That's it, I should have more *mature* things to do now. BUT I HAVEN'T!!!!!!!!

OH, DAISY, I'm going to miss you so much. For the last few months of my life, you've often been my *only friend*! THANK YOU, THANK YOU, THANK YOU AND FORGIVE ME IF YOU CAN!

5:57 p.m.

Obviously, I couldn't put you in the trash, dear Daisy. It would have been like the amputation of a major part of my body. And I truly do think I'm all right now, that I was SCARED STRAIGHT by the L'il Annie police thing. I don't know how before that I could possibly have been thinking so ... so ... irrationally.

August 20, Tuesday

Baby Annie and I are back in school, and everything is going great. It's like the sun has come out after a hard, cold winter. We've got two little baby boys and Tammy's and my little girl babies in our nursery. They're all so sweet and cuddly and full of expectations and possibilities that I can't imagine why God ever allowed four such young air-brained little kids to have them.

Oh, I almost forgot, Dr. Milshaw is setting up a special therapy group for six of us girls. I don't know why she's not having all of us, but maybe the other five don't want to come. They aren't very harmonious with the system. I . . . wish I could go alone. I'm sure the others aren't as goofed up as I am. Or are they?

August 21, Wednesday

9:47 p.m.

Went to the therapy group for unwed mothers that Dr. Milshaw suggested. There were twenty girls there instead of six, and it was like literally going to hell. I can't believe some of their stories. I don't think I'm going back; I can barely handle *my* stress and mess, so I can't see how filling my brain and soul with *their* garbage can make my situation any better or ease it the slightest.

Oh, I forgot to tell you—Gracia, an eighteen-year-old girl, and her parents, have moved into the apartment just down the hall. She's really nice, and we've gone a few places together, *but* she's got a boyfriend, and it's so wholesome and "the way it should be" that I guess I've put a big wall of some kind around myself. I can't really be *me*! But then maybe her Roger just seems like he's all the goody-goody things when he's around me and other people he wants to impress, and he's like all the other guys when the two of them are alone. Danny, at first, used to . . . But I'm trying not to think about him anymore! I'm not being very successful at it, but I am trying!

I wonder if I'm just boy-crazy, or if it's normal to want a boyfriend as much as I do. I don't mean just the . . . you-know part. . . . I mean just someone to hang in the halls with, and joke with and talk to on the phone and . . . sort of be buddy, pal, friends with, like . . . before Danny. Only tighter, but not so . . . I dunno!!!!!!!!!

I guess what I really wish I had most of all is someone to just talk to who could understand and explain but not treat me like I'm a little kid, WHICH SOMETIMES I WANT TO BE TREATED LIKE TOO.

Oh Daisy, have you ever seen anyone as mixed-up as I am?

August 22, Thursday

10:44 p.m.

I was so bored and "bummed" by Mom and everything else that I got Mrs. Abbot to baby-sit and went to another unwed mothers therapy group. It was about as gross as the other one, and when they stopped for refreshments, I said I had to go to the toilet and wandered down the hall.

I was really surprised to hear Dr. Milshaw's voice behind one of the doors, and I knocked softly, then poked my head in. She was talking on the phone and going through a stack of papers, but she motioned for me to come in and sit down, which I did gladly. Later I broke down and started crying, saying I couldn't believe how some of the girls were talking about their very own babies. That I didn't want to be any part of that kind of thing!

She got up, put her arms around me, and told me it was *good* for the girls to be able to release their negative feelings, as well as to admit having done, or felt like doing, some of the shocking, heart-crushing things I had heard; that they weren't *bad girls* just because they had had *bad feelings* during times when they were under great physical stress and emotional pain.

I totally fell apart as she told me *that* is why the therapy groups were set up. And I, who had felt I was "different" from the other girls, saw that I was not. We were all just stupid, young, naive kids who had lost our way and were now trying to *find our way back* to sanity and reality, and maybe someday, normalcy.

After a while, Dr. Milshaw compassionately led me back to the group, sat me down, kissed me on the top of the head, and went back to her work.

I listened for a while, then suddenly, like a tornado followed by a hurricane, words started spewing out of *me*! I regurgitated every disgusting thought or action I'd ever had about poor, innocent, little Baby Annie. When I had finished, it was so quiet, I opened my tear-filled eyes to see if the kids were going to "stone me" or something, but they were all crying too. In one gesture we fell into each others arms, sobbing and rejoicing at the same time! Yes! Rejoicing! All the self-anger and self-hate had been dissipated, and we were all one part of a hurting whole.

I know that sounds dumb and impossible, but it wasn't, and Lanetta, who was in charge of the group, said *NOW* we had begun to understand what a therapy group was supposed to be about.

We were all so limp from our verbal purging that Lanetta had us sit and sprawl on the floor in a circle. She joined us and became very very serious, telling us that by far, the *majority* of young unwed mothers have varied abnormal thoughts and actions, particularly if they don't have a full-time stay-at-home adult figure in their lives. She also said, with tears in her own eyes, that stress, anger, impatience, frustration, wanting to get back at the father, etc., cause innocent babies to be not only neglected, screamed at, etc., but often they are *physically abused*.

Oh, Daisy, Daisy, Daisy, I promise you with all my heart and soul that there is no way in the world I would ever hurt L'il Annie—physically, emotionally, or psychologically! You believe me don't you? Please, please say you do!

NO! DON'T! BECAUSE YOU SHOULDN'T!

Not only was there the blanket thing . . . and the police thing . . . but I've yelled at her . . . *more* than once . . . telling her to be quiet, to stop crying. . . . WORSE THAN THAT, I'VE SCREAMED AT HER TO *SHUT UP*! Mom has *never* screamed *that* at me. So what kind of a mother am I? A verbal abuser already? *What* will come next?

Both Dr. Milshaw and Lanetta have talked about adoption and have shown us charts and figures and studies, which show that *most* babies born to un-wed mothers are considered by people in the field to be, one way or another, "at risk."

NOT MY BABY! NOT MY BABY! I swear!

> *But*
> > I'm *not*
> > > Absolutely,
> > > > Totally,
> > > > > Positively
> > > > > > SURE!

Oh HELP! HELP! HELP!
> SOMEBODY PLEASE, PLEASE HELP ME!

August 23, Friday

10:22 p.m.

Mom has recognized that something is wrong with me. It's almost like I'm afraid of L'il Annie. We're going to school and everything, and I'm working very hard at doing all my extra work at an A or A+ level, but I'm sooooooo afraid of being a *bad* mother that sometimes I'm afraid to do anything at all, and I am sooooo ashamed!!!!! I know L'il Annie can't talk, but *I* still know *she knows*! And I'm not sure she can ever feel completely safe and totally secure around me in her whole life, but maybe she can, I hope!

Anyway, Mom says she's getting our bills paid

down to where pretty soon she can give up her extra job. That will make things a lot better for all of us.

Mom wants to go see Aunt Marnie this weekend and it might be fun; at least it will give us a chance to get away, or can you ever *get away* from head things?

August 25, Sunday

1:21 a.m.

This is really scary. Neither Mom nor I was comfortable around each other all weekend. I'd been looking forward to having some time with her, and then when I did, it was like . . . we were sort of strangers. And . . . in a way, I was sort of jealous of . . . well, it just seemed like she loved the baby more than she loved me. NOW ISN'T THAT STUPIDITY FOR YOU! But it seemed that way anyway, and I resented it and her and everything else. I guess I need to do some serious work on my attitude!!!!!!!!!!!!!!!!!!!!!!!!!!!
Right!

August 27, Tuesday

5:16 p.m.

I don't know whether to be excited or annoyed. Mom left a message on the answering service that she'd called a distant relative of hers, who's a shrink, and made arrangements for me to go and stay with her for a few days.

I'm really torn. I know I'm messed up and I'd like some one-on-one help, but . . . sending me away to a total stranger? I wonder if she runs a crazy farm, and if I'll be locked in with a lot of really desperate kids who have committed every crime in the book. And what about L'il Annie?

I'm getting sick to my stomach. Is Mom just trying to *get rid* of me? I'm soooo confused!!!!!

I'm supposed to be fixing dinner, and I can't remember if I salted the peas once or twice, or ten times, or not at all.

Oh, Mom, hurry, hurry, hurry home!

No matter how bad it is, let's get it over with.

I know what happened! I'll bet Mom called Dr. Milshaw and Lanetta, and they told her I was totally bonkers and needed help to *protect* L'il Annie! OH, I wouldn't hurt L'il Annie in a million years. . . . Or would I? Maybe she's sending me away for my own good *and* for Annie's.

By the time Mom got home, I was frazzled, trying to fix dinner with one hand while I held L'il Annie in the other arm. I couldn't put her down! I absolutely could not! I felt Mom was thinking of me so much as a "mini-monster mom" that she'd grab her away from me and never give her back!

Was I in for a surprise! Her relative, it turns out, is Dr. B. I had no idea *they* were related, even distantly.

I'm leaving Thursday, the 29th, and I'll come back Saturday, the 31st. It sounds almost like an adventure. Mom was getting ready to quit her second job anyway; my bag of problems just made her do it sooner instead of later. She's taking off two sick days from school, which in some crazy way makes me feel good because it will be the first days she's taken off since L'il Annie was born, and *IT'S FOR* ME! Imagine *me* coming before all the kids she teaches, and she was chosen Teacher of the Year in the state a couple of years ago! I'm getting all choked up. Imagine Mom and Dr. B. doing this for *ME*! Wow! I must be someone really important instead of the nothing, nobody I've always suspected myself of being . . . well, not always!

Mom's going to take care of L'il Annie, so I won't have a worry in creation. I can just dump and dump and dump, and heal and heal and heal . . . I hope! But . . . the scary thought keeps running through my mind that nobody can straighten up the mess in three days that I've piled up in *many*, many months, maybe most of my life.

Oooops, now I'm concentrating on my glass being half *empty* again. I think that's probably at the root of my problems, don't you? Or do you?

I better get some sleep. I've got a zillion things to do before I leave.

September 1, Sunday

9:47 a.m.

Dear Daisy Diary:

I am so, so, so, so sorry I forgot to take you with me, but as you know, L'il Annie was cross before I left, and everything else was in confusion with me not sure I should be going at the last minute and all. Anyway I'm really, really glad I went, and later I'll tell you all about my adventure, but now I'm super, super tired!!!

Oh, *before* I go, I have to tell you that Dr. B. met me at the airport with her big ex-racing greyhound dog, Newley. There was a lot of confusion and stuff, so she handed me Newley's leash while she got out her car keys. Newley came to my left side and acted like we were joined at the hip; she stayed that way almost every minute that I was at their place, even without the leash! Awesome, huh? Actually, more awesome than awesome!! I wish I could have brought her home with me. Dr. B. says Newley recognized that I was *her* relative too. *That* really made me feel comfortable and like I belonged, even though I missed L'il Annie and Mom with a kind of emptiness that I'd never known existed before.

I loved being there, but I really, really *wanted* to be home too. Thank goodness I had Newley to talk to during the long nights. She slept on my bed (I don't know if Dr. B. allowed it or not, but I didn't ask since she got up there without my inviting her to). Anyway I told her all about L'il Annie and Mom and *you*, and that helped a lot with the emptiness.

September 3, Tuesday

8:27 p.m.

I've tried really hard for two days to transcribe my tapes, and I'm about to give up. It sounded easy! NOT SO! NO WAY! Mom showed me how, but she didn't offer to do them. I guess she knew they'd be too personal; anyway, it's slow and frustrating, actually buggering! But I know I've *got* to do it. Maybe not GOT TO, but WANT TO, AND NOW THAT *I'm a mom* myself, I'm trying to be more in the "SHOULD-do-things" mode than the "WANT-to-do-things" mode. It's not easy, though! See ya later. I gotta get back to my snail-paced transcribing.

Dr. B. said *she* was in between projects and was delighted that I had come. Imagine *her* being delighted to see *me*!

We sat on Dr. B's patio down by the river and it was like . . . like *she* was *you*, Daisy. I could just sort of think out loud.

She asked me about Mom and Dad and Dad's mother, who was her something "twice removed," whatever that means. Then, I don't know how, we got to talking about me, me, me.

After a minute or two, she brought a little tape recorder out of her pocket and said if I didn't mind, she'd like to tape our conversation, so that I could listen to it later and maybe pick up things or *reinforce* positive concepts and *become aware* of negative ones that I possibly wouldn't do otherwise.

At first that made me uncomfortable, but pretty soon I forgot all about the recorder.

Tomorrow Mom's going to show me an easier way to transcribe our ten tapes to paper. I think maybe after that, I *really* will tear them up or burn them, but maybe not.

NOW!!!!!

I am *not* going to write in you again till I get all my tapes transcribed, then I think I'll put them in your book like extra pages. Tidy idea, right?

"Right."

Honestly, I really don't know what I'd do without you. Dr. B., like Mom, thinks diaries are really good things to help people put their thoughts in order and sort things out. *But* if that's true, I certainly got out of orbit for a few months in my life, with my brain turned totally on to the Superdooper Dumb Channel.

TAPE TRANSCRIPTIONS

"It's really nice to have a little second niece here, Annie. I think a second niece would be sort of like a second cousin."

"I'm happy you let me come, *whatever* I am."

"I'll tell you what you are: a wonderful, sweet, good, honorable young girl who just used poor judgement for a while."

"Did I ever! Rotten judgement that's going to follow me the rest of my life."

"Really?"

"Well, maybe not. I think I'm beginning to get things a little straightened out."

"Would you like to go back to where you first thought of yourself as getting off track?"

"Ummm. It seems so long ago it was almost like another lifetime."

"Another lifetime?"

"Yeah, one when I was young and free and believed in things . . . and myself."

"Was that a good time?"

"Oh yes! I was on the soccer team, and we had a rollerblade group that played street hockey in the park, and I had a bunch of dear girlfriends who were like . . . sisters. At least what I imagined sisters would be like. Our lives were sweet and neat.

No worries and no stress beyond surface—school, going to the mall, and other little-girl manageable stuff."

"And then?"

"Then . . . I met him."

"Does it hurt you to even say his name?"

"Yeah. It's a pain so sharp and deep that it would be *in all ways* unimaginable to people who haven't been there."

"Are you saying he was abusive?"

"Not at first. At first he was like springtime and birthdays and Christmas and the Fourth of July, and every other good thing in life tied together. He made me so happy that often I thought one more drop of joy would be beyond my ability to endure."

"Did you love him, or think you loved him?"

"Oh yes! I worshiped him from the first day I met him. He was everything I thought a boy should or could be."

"How long before . . ."

"It's really weird, but I didn't think he was abusing me until, I guess, a long time after he flushed me."

"I'm not sure what you are saying."

"I guess maybe I *can't* say it."

"I think you can."

"Well after the first party he took me to . . . he . . . he tried to rape me."

"And?"

"Something deep inside told me *then* that I shouldn't go with him any more, but that was impossible."

"Impossible?"

"Yes! Impossible!"

"Ummmmmm."

"Well, maybe not literally impossible, but . . . honestly . . . emotionally impossible! I was so . . . whatever . . . by then, I would gladly have died for him."

(Dr. B. starts talking very slowly. So slowly in fact, that I could transcribe with very little trouble.)

"I want you to stop for a minute and relax. Close your eyes and see yourself lying on a blanket with Newley, on the green lawn, under a huge oak tree. The sky is blue with just a straggle of lazy white clouds floating to your right. You feel as light and wispy and carefree as they look. Far off, you can hear birds singing, bees buzzing lazily, and a little brook meandering slowly over some rocks. You can smell wild roses and feel sunbeams squishing their way through the softly, slowly blowing leaves to rest lightly and warmly on your cheek. Newley moves slightly and rests one paw on your stomach. Life is cool and serenely relaxed, beautiful, and well worth living.

"Before you open your eyes, start slowly thinking about what you MIGHT have done *after* that first experience. Remain relaxed and in charge of your mental processes."

"I guess I could have . . . *should* have talked to someone, but that would have been tough because Mom didn't want me to date till I was sixteen, and I was only fourteen, and . . . all my friends were fourteen, too, and dumb as I. I'm thinking now how dumb and lucky and innocent and uncluttered and irresponsible their lives *still* probably are."

"What do you think your mom would have done if you had talked to her?"

"She'd have lectured and preached and warned and grounded me for forever . . . and who knows what else."

"Oh."

"Actually she's not that way at all. *I'm* just being paranoid because, I guess, I *still* don't want to fully accept responsibility for *my* actions. I know as well as I'm sitting here that I should have talked with her instead of . . ."

(Very long pause.)

"Instead of what?"

"Making a complete jackass fool of myself by . . . wanting him to be my boyfriend so much, I tried to take all the blame for *his* actions on myself! I felt I'd do anything, ANYTHING to get him back, *and I dumbly did.*

"I didn't care that he treated me disrespectfully and cruelly, physically, mentally, emotionally, and . . . you know. It was like my brains had been turned off, and my hormones had been turned on! I can't . . . I simply can't believe I did the things I did."

(I started crying like a dam inside me had broken.)

"It's okay sweetie, sometimes people, especially young people, don't realize that the urge to procreate can be one of the strongest drives on earth, that *it* is what keeps life continuing! *However, important as it is, it* must be controlled, like fire, atomic energy, etc."

"I'm learning that a little late."

"Did you think you loved . . ."

"Danny."

"Did you honestly think that you *loved* Danny?"

"I . . . loved him more than anything on earth."

"What is love?"

"It's . . . it's . . . Is it when someone else is more important than *you* are?"

"Does that seem . . . and feel . . . right to you?"

"Well . . . not exactly somehow, but . . ."

"I'm going to give you a little self-quiz about love; I give it to many of the people I work with. Read it when you're alone and quiet. And we'll talk about it later if you want to."

WHAT IS LOVE?

Does the person I think I love:	Always	Sometimes	Rarely	Never
Make me feel happy?				
Make me feel important?				
Make me feel attractive?				
Make me feel kinder?				
Make me feel smarter?				
Make me nicer to myself and others?				
Make me feel valued?				
Make me feel comfortable with myself?				
Make me feel comfortable with others?				
Make me feel proud of what I am doing?				
Make me feel proud of who I am?				
Make me feel of benefit to him?				

Does the person I think I love:

	Always	Sometimes	Rarely	Never
Try to control me?				
Think I am *wrong* if I don't agree?				
Want everything his way?				
Make me feel ashamed?				
Make me feel embarrassed?				
Make me feel afraid?				
Make me feel insecure?				

Does the person I think I love HURT me:

	Always	Sometimes	Rarely	Never
Physically?				
Mentally?				
Emotionally?				
Socially?				
Scholastically?				
With my friends?				
With my family?				

Would he AT ALL TIMES:

	Always	Sometimes	Rarely	Never
Protect me?				
Cherish me?				
Encourage me?				
Build me?				

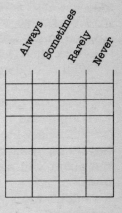

Does he ALWAYS:

	Always	Sometimes	Rarely	Never
Bring out the best in me?				
Care deeply about my concerns?				
Put my needs on as high a priority as his own?				
Have faith in my abilities and suggestions?				
Stand up for me?				

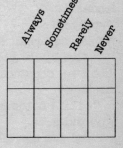

	Always	Sometimes	Rarely	Never
ARE "TRUE, LASTING LOVE" AND "RESPECT" ONE?				
DOES HE TREAT ME WITH RESPECT?				

AFTER DINNER

Dr. B.: "Do you want to talk, or would you rather watch TV for a while?"

"I've got so many questions, they're blowing around in my head like a cyclone."

"Quick then, let's answer some of them."

"Well . . . I'd never really been with a boy before Danny. Oh, lots of us used to hang out together in the mall and at school and stuff, but . . ."

(Long pause.)

"But what? I told you in the car coming here that anything, *positively anything* that you talk with me about will *always* be absolutely, sacredly secret."

"I don't want you to think I'm . . ."

"I don't!"

"There is soooooooooooo much I'm mixed up about."

"Like?"

"Is it all right for guys to . . . hit girls?"

"*Absolutely not!* If a boy hits you, it shows he not only *does not respect* you, he *does not respect* himself!"

"I . . . I hated it, but . . . I guess I thought every guy did it."

"Believe me, *EVERY* guy does not!"

"But all the guys in our crowd . . ."

"The old 'EVERYBODY'S DOING IT' is one of the world's biggest fallacies. If everyone in *your* crowd is doing it, it may seem like everyone else is too, but that isn't necessarily so. Kids who tag think 'everyone does it'; kids who are brought up in abnormal homes think ABNORMALITY IS NORMAL! Kids who are into any kind of deviate behavior often honestly think it is much more rampant than it is."

"What . . . what about . . ."

"About?"

"Rough . . ."

"Rough sex?"

"Yeah."

"Anyone who inflicts pain upon another person is sadistic. You're looking at me quickly—do you know what sadistic means?"

"Sort of, but . . ."

"Sadism means getting sexual pleasure from dominating, mistreating, or hurting someone else physically or otherwise."

"Danny said . . ."

"What?"

"I was so stupid and gullible and naive, I can't believe I . . ."

"Do you want to talk about it?"

"No, but I wish I knew how come boys don't have to take any responsibility for anything they do. It doesn't seem fair or right or anything. Of all the girls I knew who went to our Unwed Mothers school, only one of them had any help, and that was because the girl's father made the two guys pay for her two abortions. Probably both of them would have skipped or something if they'd thought they had to pay child support or whatever, for forever."

"There are some interesting changes happening in our laws right now. California's governor and the state's prosecutor are stepping up enforcement of statutory rape laws against men who impregnate underage girls."

"You said *men*, and I guess it is *usually* older guys, at least it was in our UWM school. I think there were only a couple of us who had boyfriends about our own age; actually, even Danny was two years older than me."

"A study in the *American Journal of Public Health* states that two thirds of the babies born to teenage mothers in California were fathered by adult men who were, on average, four to six years older than the girls. The article also stated that U.S. teenagers give birth to more than *a million* babies every year, and that the younger the mother, the greater the age gap. Girls in high school had babies with men who were on average 4.2 years older, while junior high girls bore children by men on average 6.7 years older."

"That's scary, and it seems like *nobody* (sniff, sniff), including me, is ever thinking about a little, unguilty child when they're . . . doing it."

"Maybe they should, and maybe if *all* males knew they were going to have to take *their* share of the responsibility in a pregnancy, by being either a 'child-rearer' or a 'time-doer,' they might take sexual accountability more seriously."

"I don't think anyone in Danny's and my crowd thought anything about consequences, at least it certainly wasn't number one in our minds."

"And it's about time serious thought is given to the subject, isn't it? In California alone the state and federal taxpayers spend *$7 billion* annually for welfare and health care benefits for families started by TEENS."

"To say nothing about all the poor little innocent, mostly unwanted babies that . . . Do you think it's true that all babies born to teenagers are 'at risk'? "

"Probably *most* of them are."

"I didn't want to believe that."

"Think about it—how many of you young girls would know if your baby had an earache, if she was teething, if she had an upset stomach, if she was getting enough to eat, if her formula or breast milk was agreeing with her, if she was warm enough or cool enough, what to do about rashes or runny noses or mucus around her eyes, or diarrhea, or dehydration? More babies in the world die of dehydration than of any other one thing."

"I DON'T WANT TO HEAR ANY MORE! . . . but I do, too; I should; I've got to."

"You're sure?"

"I'm sure."

"Well, the National Centers for Disease Control data inform us that the out-of-wedlock birth rate has doubled in the past few years. That the national average is more than 31 percent. The highest rate is in Washington, D.C., where 67 percent of births are out of wedlock. Mississippi, Louisiana, and New Mexico follow with 44.4 percent."

"What is the answer?"

"A whole collection of *values!*"

"What about protection?"

"I'm sure you are aware that while condoms are touted as being *the* answer, THEY DO NOT *guarantee* anyone 100 percent protection. They *do* give *some* protection, and if people are going to be sexually active, they certainly should wear them, as well as using spermicidal jelly, which still does not present a 100 percent safety net 100 percent of the time."

"What about those little thingies they put in a girl's arm?"

"If a girl *is* going to be sexually active, she *should*, from the beginning, consider the possibility of bringing an unwanted child into a hostile environment, and seriously consider Depo-Provera shots, which last for about three months, or Norplant, a small implant in her upper arm, so simple that it can be inserted by a nurse through an incision so small it can hardly be seen."

"How long will a Norplant keep a girl sterile?"

"Up to five years."

"Someone told me they were dangerous, that they could make you not able to have children even when you got old enough to maybe really want them."

"That is not true."

"I know that I've learned my lesson the hard way, and *I'm* going to stay celibate."

"Just so you won't get pregnant?"

"No . . . because it's right for me! It's part of *my* value system. Always has been, but I've heard that once you've been sexually active, you *can't* stop. I don't think I believe that."

"I definitely don't."

"That makes me happy. I suspect I've heard a

lot of untrue garbage in the last few months, stuff I'm going to dump far, far out of my life."

"Good for you. I'm proud of you! Proud that you're my kin and proud that you're my friend."

Newley poked one paw through the little crack in the door, pushed it open, came in, and curled up beside my chair with her head on my feet. We *were* family! A good, clean, honorable, *virtuous* family. I now have my head on straight and I AM GOING TO KEEP IT THAT WAY THROUGH ALL THE ETERNITIES OF THE ETERNITIES!

I know I said I was going to transcribe all Dr. B's tapes, but I can't. It's too time-consuming, and besides *you're* really *me*, so you know them anyway. Guess we'll just have to go on from here, except I want to tell you one more thing Dr. B and I talked about that I think is an awesomely needed concept.

Some schools have a "Baby Think-It-Over Doll" that they pass around to their kids over weekends. It's made of soft, plasticized rubber and looks and sounds like a real six-pound infant.

When kids first see it, even the boys want to play with it. It's cute and cuddly, but it's computerized to cry when it dislikes its position, needs feeding or tending, wants to sleep, or has been handled too roughly. And it *electronically records* whether its "parent" has responded, or has, even by shaking or dropping it, committed child abuse.

At first, most students are enthusiastic about their new charge. But both boys and girls, after repeatedly getting up in the middle of the night to quiet cries that come in intervals stretching from fifteen minutes to six hours, get the message pretty soon that babies are a lot of work.

Often students deemed at high risk of pregnancy, those with low self-esteem and poor academic performance, are given cranky dolls that cry from every fifteen minutes to an hour and a half. It can take up to twenty minutes to stop the nerve-wracking wailing. One girl said she wanted to throw it out the window. And boys admitted they'd wanted to dump it in a closet, so they could get some sleep, or really scary thoughts ran through their minds, like putting it in a plastic bag or smashing it. Sleep deprivation was the kids' biggest complaint, and they didn't even have the diaper-changing and the bathing and washing and drying and folding clothes and cleaning and feeding, and on and on forever, day and night things.

I wish *I'd* had the program because I had NO IDEA until . . . but there's nothing we can do about that now, especially since L'il Annie started crying this very moment, and I'm soooooooooooo tired, I want the sound to go away . . . I want her to go away. Far, far, forever away—but not really—I guess.

1:16 a.m.

I finally got L'il Annie to sleep. Mom came in and helped me rock her, walk the floor with her, give her some warm water in a bottle, pat her belly, rub her back, and everything else we could think of, or that the baby book suggested.

I've still got lessons to do that I thought I'd get up early and do in the morning, but it's morning now and I haven't *yet* gone to sleep. Actually, now I'm so sleepy, I *can't* go to sleep. But I guess I can. I better try anyway.

L'il Annie was cross all day in school, and everybody was mad at me. She woke up the other three babies in the nursery room and eardrum-pierced all eight of the other students. Finally even the teacher couldn't stand it any longer. Actually she tried to use L'il Annie's crying as an object lesson to the whole class—and explained gently, over the bedlam (because the other babies were by then crying), that this is what babies do. That one of the toughest things about babies is that there really are no blanket solutions to crying, etc. That sometimes no matter what you do, you can't fix the problem, a fact that is triplely frustrating to teenagers. Then she suggested maybe I should take L'il Annie home.

Using my baby as the example was a completely humiliating experience! Who would ever have dreamed that conformist, good-grade me would ever get kicked out of school because my baby cried.

I was feeling pretty negative and defeated until about halfway home when L'il Annie's tense, tiny body relaxed, and she curled up in my arms and, making precious little sounds, went to sleep looking and feeling like a soft, warm, sweet-smelling angel. I gently touched the skin on her hand and face and again marveled that it was like no other soft substance on earth.

I'm amazed that sometimes I can feel such wondrous devotion to this innocent little part of my body and soul, and that other times . . . I . . . I . . . *I've never hated her*; I just resent the time and effort and everything she takes. I guess I'm just having trouble coexisting with my mixed, childish, dumb feelings right?

October 1, Tuesday

9:10 p.m.

I know I haven't written you for a couple of weeks, but not only is L'il Annie sick, I think I am too. I'm having diarrhea and throwing up a lot. I don't want Mom to know because we've got enough to worry about with L'il Annie. She's got a fever that even the antibiotics don't seem to help. I'm worried, worried, worried about her and feel so responsible for her being this way that I can't get much down my throat, and when I do get something down, it comes right up—or *out*—in just a few minutes.

A home teacher is coming twice a week, but I don't feel like studying. In fact, I honestly can't comprehend why I was so dead set on graduating high school at seventeen. That seems pointless now; in fact, everything's of no consequence, except Annie. I'm afraid to be out of her sight, afraid to sleep, even afraid of taking long showers. What if something happened to her?

I haven't been out of the apartment for the two weeks that L'il Annie has been sick, except the times we took her to the doctor, and I've lost so much weight that I have to put a big safety pin in the back of my pants and wear my shirts outside. Mom is so busy, she hasn't noticed except to tell me I look pale.

I really feel rotten, and I hate to admit this, but ... I'm jealous of L'il Annie. I *used to get* love and attention and tender loving care, now ... now I'm just lonely, frightened, exhausted, depressed, *really, really* depressed.

Cinderella Annie ... *with no Fairy Godmother* to come save me.

October 2, Wednesday

7:59 p.m.

Mom came home from school and found me fainted on the floor just outside the bathroom. I don't know how she brought me out of it, but Mrs. Turner, who lives down the hall, came to sit with L'il Annie while Mom took me to the doctor. He said it was mainly being run down and exhausted. Mom was tense about me, but I didn't care about myself. I was only concerned about L'il Annie. Mrs. Turner is sooooooooooooo old, I wasn't sure she'd remember what to do from the way-back time when she had her kids.

October 4, Friday

9:45 p.m.

I'm back in my old routine, but I am soooooooooooo tired and drained all the time. After getting L'il Annie and myself ready for school and feeding us, I'm ready to go back to bed. Anyway, life goes on . . . but barely. Dr. Milshaw talked to me for a while after lunch. She thinks I'm depressed, but I'm not; I'm just tired, all-the-time, to-the-bone tired.

I'm scared about Mom too. She's so busy taking care of me and the baby that she doesn't have time to take care of herself. I dread to think what would happen if anything happened to *her*.

October 5, Saturday

6:45 p.m.

I love L'il Annie with all my heart. I adore her! But I find all that is expected of me is harder and harder to handle each day!!!! Last night I dreamed I was a little teeny kid myself, going down life's slippery,

slippery slide ... slowly, slowly going down, down, down, though I was trying to hold onto each side with my hands and by bracing my feet. It was scary and exhausting. I wonder if it meant something; dreams sometimes do. Maybe I'll get a dream book from the library, but probably not; it's too much trouble.

9:20 p.m.

I know Mom's worried about me, even though I try my hardest to be cheery and keep my part of the house and the baby up and everything. She's a good mom.

I'm trying really hard to do everything Dr. B. suggested about keeping my attitude positive and my energy level up, but. . . . Sorry, just got the baby down; think I'll go to bed myself.

October 6, Sunday

11:49 p.m.

Dearest, dearest confidante and friend:

You won't believe what happened. Right after dinner, Bishop Marden, from the church that Mom and I have gone to a few times, came by. Actually, Mom had called because she was so worried about me and L'il Annie, and . . . I guess, everything. Anyway, Bishop Marden was so . . . so much like a kind, wise grandfather that I could see little kids laughing and climbing on his knee and playing horsey on his bucking foot, and all those things that little kids need.

He stayed for a long time and Mom fixed her special banana and frozen strawberry and orange juice blender drink, and we talked about Annie and me and "unplanned pregnancies" that happen to very good, good girls. It took him and Mom a while to convince me that I *was one of them*, but I finally believed it. I really do! I'm not the—all the things Danny said I was—I am just one of the dumb, immature kids who made some very, very, very stupid choices that I'm going to have to live with for the rest of my life.

Bishop Marden told us about his son and daughter and their families. How much they love each other and work and play, and laugh and tease, and sometimes *bicker* together. He said the disagreeing was a very normal part of life's problem-solving program if it's handled without people losing control.

As he talked, a part of me realized how much L'il Annie would be missing by not having a real father—I haven't seen mine in a couple of years— or a grandfather, or . . . I started crying, and they both comforted me like I was the little kid I really still am in many ways.

Bishop Marden gently told me to be superkind and considerate of myself until I have adjusted to my new role, and more emotional healing has taken place. Then he started talking about adoption so lovingly and sacredly . . . YES, SACREDLY! that my heart bleeds for the sad, lonely, grown-up couples who love each other and aren't blessed with the cooing sounds and smells and feels of a baby.

He told us of one couple he knew, actually fairly distant relatives of his, who had longed and prepared and prayed for children all the seven years of their marriage. He even showed us a beautiful picture of them and their big dog, which had a smile on its face that reminded me of Newley. When Bishop Marden finally told us good night, he reminded us again that he would *always* be available if we needed him.

Mom and I both wanted to stop him, but instead we fell into each other's arms and talked for almost five hours, about the pros and cons of allowing L'il Annie the privilege of living with the complete, mature, full family that is part of Bishop Marden's huge, mature, extended family. He hadn't mentioned *it* himself, but . . . how could I ever part with L'il Annie? It would be like giving up part of my body and my soul. . . . I don't know much about souls . . . but I know there's *something beyond* what *I* know! *Something* important and powerful and eternally *omnipotent*! I don't even know what the word means, but I heard it once and it *feels* right!!!!!!!!!!!!!!

8:21 p.m.

Mom and I met Bishop Marden's relatives. They're a beautiful young couple, in fact he has my hair and face coloring, and she has my light brown eyes. Mom says they're "gold." Steve calls his wife Jo-Jo (her name is really Josephine) *"Golden Eyes"* because her eyes are light brown too. Isn't that strange?

And another thing strange, L'il Annie was crying when I picked her up, but as soon as Jo-Jo held her with Steve goo-gooing over her shoulder, the little stinker started smiling and drooling. It was like an omen or something, but not really! I AM *NOT* GOING TO GIVE HER UP!

10:31 p.m.

Mom and I talked for another couple of hours, and I'm soooooooo confused. I want L'il Annie to have all the love and security and normalcy that Steve and Jo-Jo can give her, but still I'm sure I'll just wither away and die, and I'll forever feel guilty and like I've committed *two* major sins instead of one! I wish I knew how to pray. I remember when I was teeny-tiny, Mom took me to Sunday School for a while; then Dad didn't want her to anymore. I wonder why not? Why *didn't* he want me and Mom to do *lots* of things we wanted to do? I guess maybe that means I didn't really have an exactly normal childhood, and I *want* L'il Annie to have one! I really truly do! I do, but I *DON'T*! I won't give her up . . . yet how can I, a barely fifteen-year-old kid . . . I know Mom will help, but she's got a life of her own. I wish, though, that she'd tell me what to do! But she said it had to be *my* decision. I know she'll support me a million percent and I suspect she thinks . . . Jo-Jo and Steve both love the names Mary Ann and L'il Annie, and we've seen pictures of their house, and he is SO STABLE AND KIND, and he treats Jo-Jo like she's the smartest, nicest, most perfect thing in the world, and she loves and respects him the same way. It's exactly the way a nice family should be. I wouldn't want Mom to know this, but it's like the one I wish I had grown up in, instead of us living in that dingy one-room apartment while Mom finished getting her teaching credentials. It was so scary and dangerous there that neither one of us dared go out after the sun went down.

Thinking about *that*, I've got to be realistic and consider what would happen to L'il Annie and me if something happened to Mom. What if she got married again in the next year or so? No way would her new husband want to be saddled with a baby and a *mother kid*. I wish I . . . I don't even know what to wish. I want L'il Annie to be taught ethics, to have good role models—but from still-little-kid me? I'm not sure. . . .

January 7, Tuesday

Dear Daisy Diary:
   I've been weeping from loneliness, guilt, and pain for three months, but I know in my heart . . . at least, sometimes I think I know in my heart, that it was right to allow L'il Annie the *opportunity* to grow up in an normal adult home with normal adult parents, who love her and also respect and love each other. But I hurt so much, I honestly didn't know anyone could hurt this much and not die. I don't think I could make it without . . . I'm not sure I *am* going to make it.
   Often I feel L'il Annie's soft little fist burrowing its way down into my fist, and I miss her nuzzling and cooing and baby hugs so much that there are not enough hurtful words in the world to express it. And at night sometimes I wake up feeling so empty that I'm just a dead shell of what used to be a living creature. OH, I do hope I won't always and forever feel this empty, dark, lonely, incomplete, totally useless, totally expendable way. I guess I've got to dwell more on what, in the overall picture, *is right for Annie*!!!!! Yes! That's the only thing I can do. I'm sure . . . well, almost sure, that that's what

God wants me to do! I wish—I honestly, truly, absolutely, for sure knew . . . whatever.

January 9, Thursday

6:23 p.m.

Mom bounced in about an hour ago, like a little five-year-old kid. She had a torn-open letter in her hand and was gushing and laughing and stumbling over words until I wondered for a minute if *she* had had a nervous breakdown instead of me. Finally she collapsed on the floor, dragging me down beside her, and told me that she had received an offer to be the *vice principal* at a fancy, high-paying, respected private school upstate.

"You, a vice principal," I giggled. "The kids will eat you alive, you twinky."

She wrestled me over her knee and tickled me, then gave me a few swats on the rear. "That's what I'll do to them too, even the biggest jocks if they get mouthy with me."

We scuffled for a while, teasing and tittering like we hadn't done in a forever of forevers. It was wonderful, and I knew for the first time since . . . you know, that I truly *could* make it.

January 27, Monday

6:32 a.m.

Before I take the last box out to the car and trem-
blingly tiptoe into my new life, I must take one last-
time look at the two hearts I carved on the big old
weeping willow tree behind our apartment com-
plex the day after my first meeting with Danny on
the junior high school soccer field.

for the past will forever be a part of my present and my future!

Questions From Teenagers About Pregnancy and STDs (Sexually Transmitted Diseases)

"Can I get pregnant the first time?"

Yes, if you are in the fertile part of your menstrual cycle.

"A girl at my school says she got pregnant and she didn't even really . . . you know . . . 'do it.' That's not possible is it?"

Yes, it is possible for a girl to get pregnant without intercourse. *One drop of semen* (the fluid secreted by the male reproductive organs) can contain as many as 50,000 sperm. If the semen touches the vulva (the external, visible part of the female sexual organs) only one of these aggressive swimmers needs to wiggle its way up the vagina (the muscular passage forming part of the female reproductive system) and through the cervix. Then we have a case like the girl you mentioned.

"Does that happen a lot?"

Chances are *against it* because it is some distance from the vulva to the uterus (where the baby grows). Young people may *feel* safer "fooling around" instead of having intercourse, but that is a false sense of security, since the odds of a renegade sperm getting loose are directly based on the number of exposures.

"How effective is it to . . . take the penis out before the guy comes?"

The risk of pregnancy is *great*. Even *before* ejaculation there is a chance that a drop or two of semen will be secreted, and remember each drop can contain about 50,000 sperm.

"How safe is 'safe sex' with condoms?"

Not one hundred percent. Even using a latex condom with a spermicide is not one hundred percent safe one hundred percent of the time. Of one hundred women whose partners always use condoms, about twelve will become pregnant during the first year of typical use, *if* the condom is used correctly. Sometimes *it isn't*, as all users know. The medical field considers condoms an "unreliable barrier" against pregnancy.

"How safe is the birth control pill?"

Of one hundred women taking the birth control pill for a year and using it according to directions, three may become pregnant.

"What about Norplant? How safe is it?"

Norplant is 99.96 percent effective. A clinician puts six small capsules (shorter than toothpicks and a little bit thicker) under the skin in the girl's upper arm. The capsules constantly release small amounts of hormones that prevent the discharge of eggs from the ovaries and thicken cervical mucus to keep sperm from joining the egg. The Norplant can be removed at any time by a clinician. It protects against pregnancy for five years but is not effective against any sexually transmitted diseases. It costs about five hundred dollars and is covered by some insurance policies.

"Tell me about the shot."

Depo-Provera is a shot that will keep you from getting pregnant for twelve weeks. The shot contains a hormone that keeps the female's eggs from leaving her ovaries. It also thickens the mucus at the opening of the uterus so the male's sperm cannot get inside. About three out of one thousand women who use the shot for a year get pregnant. Depo-Provera *does not protect* against AIDS or other STDs.

"How many sexually transmitted diseases are there? Are they hard to get?"

There are more than twenty STDs and most are easy to get. Actually more than *three million* (one out of four) sexually active teens are affected by sexual diseases each year. A few of these are chlamydia (which can cause sterility), syphilis (which can cause blindness, death, and death to the infant if an infected woman has a baby), herpes II (related to the cold sore people get on their lips, has no cure and is recurring), and AIDS (which is eventually fatal to the mother and can be to an infant).

In a single act of unprotected sex with an infected partner, a teenage girl has a one percent risk of acquiring HIV, a thirty percent risk of getting genital herpes, and a fifty percent chance of contracting gonorrhea. Use of a condom every time a man and a woman have sex reduces the risk of contracting an STD from a sexual partner. It is the only reliable way to reduce the risk.

"What if you're raped?"

Anyone, boy or girl, should get to a phone as soon as possible. Call 911, the police, or your local Rape Crisis Center. DO NOT BATHE, WASH, CHANGE YOUR CLOTHES, GO TO THE BATHROOM, DRINK ANYTHING OR BRUSH YOUR TEETH.

"Why?"

Because semen is as identifiable as fingerprints and there may be traces in your mouth as well as on your clothes or elsewhere on your body.

"If I went to a clinic or hospital immediately after, would that keep me from getting pregnant or AIDS or something?"

Yes and no. The nurse or doctor would give you medication to prevent pregnancy and they can also prescribe antibiotics that fight some sexually transmitted diseases. However, AIDS and herpes II cannot, at this time, be controlled by ANY MEDICATIONS.

"Do teenage moms have more troubles with pregnancy?"

Yes. A teenage mother is much more at risk of pregnancy complications such as premature or prolonged labor, anemia, toxemia, high blood pressure, and miscarriage. These risks are even greater for teens who are less than fifteen years old.

"Do teen moms' babies have more problems?"

Yes. A baby born to a teen mother is more at risk than a baby born to an older mother. A large percentage of teenage girls have low birth weight babies (less than 5½ pounds). These babies often have organs that are not fully developed, as well as lung problems, mental retardation, difficulty controlling body temperature and sugar levels, and other problems. They are forty times more likely than normal weight babies to die in their first month of life.

"I'm very mature for fifteen. Why can't my sex life be MY decision?"

It is your decision! That is why I, as an adolescent psychologist and *great respecter* of young adults, am asking you to carefully consider the CONSE-QUENCES of teenage pregnancy. More than a million girls get pregnant each year in the United States and over half a million give birth. The others have abortions or miscarriages. Fifteen percent of teens who get pregnant will be pregnant again within one year and twenty five percent of teenage mothers have a second child within two years of their first.

Two out of three pregnant teenagers drop out of school with no job skills. It is the major cause of school dropouts among girls.

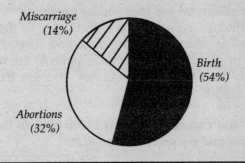

TEEN PREGNANCIES
1 million teenage pregnancies each year

Miscarriage
(14%)

Birth
(54%)

Abortions
(32%)

"I don't want to hear any more . . . but . . . maybe I should. . . . I'd like to know how I'd go about getting welfare for me and my kid if I do get . . . or I am . . . pregnant."

IT'S NOT AS EASY AS IT USED TO BE! In January 1997 the government disbanded *welfare* and replaced it with a new, tougher program called FEP (Family *Employment* Program), which says *no one* is *entitled* to something for nothing.

"How can they do that?"

Probably because the old AFDC program (Aid for Families of Dependent Children) cost the Untied States government $25 BILLION A YEAR!—mostly for families begun by teen births.

"So what are we going to do now?"

FEP guidelines say if you are under eighteen years old YOUR PARENTS are going to have to be responsible for you.

"What about the guy that got me pregnant?"

On the old program the ORS (Office of Recovery Service) would go after the male you named as the father of your baby. Now your parents are responsible to the ORS for any money you get from the government.

"But I don't want me and my kid to have to live with my mom and my second stepdad."

Unless you can afford to live on your own and pay your own bills, you may have no other choice.

"Well . . . if that's the only way. I guess I'll just have to get Mom and Jeffery to go in and get the benefits for me."

Your parents probably won't want to do that because every cent they get *for you* they will have to pay back in full. *YOU* can apply for PN (prenatal medical care) but basically that is all that will be *given* to you.

"That's not fair. My mom used to be on welfare before she married Jeffery and her parents were on it, too."

And so were thousands of others, but no more! Welfare as your mom knew it doesn't exist today. FEP has taken its place and *it* is *not* an *entitlement* program, meaning people no longer have a *right* to *"get something for nothing."*

"That's scary. What if my mom won't . . . what-ever."

Actually, people should be happy about the government's new Family Employment Program. It sounds complicated but it's really very simple and in the long run helpful.

1. You (anyone) can apply for assistance.
2. You'll have a two-hour session with a case manager and together you'll work up a plan, including:
   a. short term goals to get your GED if possible
   b. work training to teach you job skills
   c. *a job*, and possibly some subsidized child care

"In the meantime, who is going to pay for the baby's formula and diapers and stuff?"

YOU are going to be responsible for yourself and your child, hopefully with some parental help. You might be eligible for three hundred forty-three dollars per month for both you and your baby on this program but that would require you to go to school and work for a grant. That means *hard work*, commitment, and growing up fast with more responsibilities than you've ever dreamed of. Also, you (anyone) are allowed only thirty-six months (three years) out of your entire lifetime on this program, unlike THE OLD WELFARE PROGRAM WHEN SOME FAMILIES WERE ON IT FOR GENERATIONS.

Statistics

Out-of-wedlock births more than doubled between 1986 and 1996. Birth rates are now declining, but the decline is not consistent; *among those fourteen or younger the birth rate is increasing*!

The national average of out-of-wedlock births is thirty-six percent (more than one-third of all births). The highest rate is in Washington, D.C., where sixty-seven percent of births are out-of-wedlock. Mississippi, Louisiana, and New Mexico have forty-five percent. Only Utah, Texas, and Idaho rate under twenty percent.

- Sixty percent of teen pregnancies occur during the first six months of sexual activity.
- Among teens unmarried at the time of childbirth more than sixty-five percent go on welfare within three years.
- The divorce rate is greater for couples with a pre-marital pregnancy than for those who conceive after marriage.
- Teens are more likely than older women to delay abortions until the second three months of pregnancy, when health risks associated with an abortion increase significantly.

- *More than eighty percent of pregnant teens are unmarried*. The younger the girl, the higher the percentage.
- Sixty percent of teenage mothers give birth to babies fathered by men age twenty or older.
- The younger the girl, the greater the age difference.
- In the United States, unwed mothers give birth to approximately 1,240,000 (*one million*, two hundred and forty thousand) children *each year*. Approximately three percent of these children are placed for adoption while ninety-seven percent are kept by the single mother.
- Time and studies have shown that adoption, difficult though it may be for the young mother, often affords a child a greater opportunity to live a life of security and happiness.

  Most young unwed mothers do not know that one-sixth of married couples in the United States experience infertility and rely on adoption to receive a baby. Ten to twelve percent of couples are eventually able to adopt a child.
- Unwed mothers who keep their children are more likely to remain unmarried and to have children who experience pregnancy out of wedlock.
- Children raised by unwed parents are more often abused, are two to three times as likely to have serious emotional and behavior problems, and are more likely to drop out of high school and to be in trouble with the law.

Violence

One in eight girls will experience abuse in a relationship during high school. It can be obvious—shoving, slapping, punching, or:

- threats or verbal abuse
- forcing a girl to go farther sexually than she wants to
- demeaning remarks, which lower self-identity
- controlling actions which restrict a girl's free agency

IF *ANY* GIRL IS BEING ABUSED,
SHE SHOULD NOT IGNORE IT OR
SUFFER QUIETLY.
SHE SHOULD GET HELP!
IT IS AS CLOSE AS HER TELEPHONE.
CALL A CRISIS LINE, RAPE CENTER,
SCHOOL COUNSELOR;
*TALK TO AN ADULT WHO IS
KNOWLEDGEABLE AND TRUSTWORTHY.*
"EVERYBODY *ISN'T* DOING IT!"

Crisis or Information Hotline Numbers

1-800 means they are free of cost.

Where to call for Abuse, Assault, or Rape Information

Call your local RAPE CRISIS LINE or your local CRISIS LINE; they will be listed in the phone book and will answer your questions and get help for you. If your town is so small it does not have a crisis line listed, call 1-800-656-HOPE (4673), or the police. If you call the HOPE LINE, no matter where you live, they will route your call *to a local help line!* You can also call the Sexual Assault Crisis Line at 1-800-643-6250.

Where to call for Pregnancy Information

Call your local CRISIS LINE, 1-800-230-PLAN (7526), Planned Parenthood, or the Pregnancy Risk Hotline for BABY YOUR BABY at 1-800-822-2229, and the Emergency Contraception Hotline at 1-800-584-9911. The National Hotline for Pregnant Women can be reached at 1-800-311-BABY.

Where to call for
Sexually Transmitted Disease Information

Call your local CRISIS LINE or 1-800-227-8922. They will answer all your questions and/or refer you to free or low-cost clinics in your area.

Either of the numbers will tell you where you can get health examinations, pregnancy testing, counseling, infection treatments, and other information.

For information on AIDS and HIV, call the national AIDS Hotline at 1-800-342-2437. ASK A NURSE at 1-800-535-1111 has information for teens and adults about health matters.

Where to call for Information Related to
Suicidal Feelings

Your local CRISIS LINE, 1-800-230-7526, 1-800-822-2229, or 911. Talk to someone who is knowledgeable about the subject. They can dilute your stress and fears as well as help you find answers and solutions to your problems. There is a way out ! You just need someone to help you find it!

What about talking to your parents, a school counselor or a church leader? They are all there to help you.

Abstinence

The United States government, Bureau of Maternal and Child Health, is in the process of funding an abstinence outreach program to every state in the union. The grants will be administered by each state through its individual state health department.

Material Sources

- Centers for Disease Control (CDC)
- March of Dimes
- Baby Think It Over
- Baby Net
- Alan Guttmacher Institute
- Planned Parenthood
- ERIC/CAPS Fact Sheet
- Social Services
- Family Health Service National

Thanks to all of the above; also, "Annie," her mother, her friends, her teachers, Linda Gustin from our local Social Service office, my husband and family who are so patient about my writing, and you, the reader. You are a part of my life as I hope *ANNIE* will be a part of yours.

BEATRICE SPARKS prepared for publication the bestseller *Go Ask Alice*, along with *It Happened to Nancy* and others. She has been working as a professional counselor with "hurting" kids for many years and has conducted therapy groups and special seminars around the country. She *loves* and *listens* to kids, and they in return "love, trust, and feel safe" with her.

Beatrice Sparks holds a Doctorate of Philosophy in Human Behavior. Her books have won the Christopher Medal and have been named as School Library Journal Best Books, Notable Books, and Quick Picks for Recommended Reading by the American Library Association.

Dr. Sparks was a 1996 National Book Awards Judge for Young People's Literature.

Gripping, true-life accounts
for today's teens

Edited by
Beatrice Sparks, Ph.D.

IT HAPPENED TO NANCY
She thought she'd found love…
but instead lost her life to AIDS.
77315-5/$4.99 US/$6.99 Can

ALMOST LOST
The True Story
of an Anonymous Teenager's
Life on the Streets
782841-X/$4.99 US/$6.99 Can

ANNIE'S BABY
The Diary of Anonymous,
A Pregnant Teenager
79141-2/$4.99 US/$6.99 Can

Thought-Provoking Novels
from Today's Headlines

HOMETOWN
by Marsha Qualey   72921-0/$3.99 US/$4.99 Can
Border Baker isn't happy about moving to his father's rural
Minnesota hometown, where they haven't forgotten that
Border's father fled to Canada rather than serve in Vietnam.
Now, as a new generation is bound for the Persian Gulf, the
town wonders about the son of a draft dodger.

NOTHING BUT THE TRUTH
by Avi   71907-X/$4.99 US /$6.99 Can
Philip was just humming along with *The Star Spangled
Banner*, played each day in his homeroom. How could this
minor incident turn into a major national scandal?

TWELVE DAYS IN AUGUST
by Liza Ketchum Murrow   72353-0/$3.99 US/$4.99 Can
Sixteen-year-old Todd is instantly attracted to Rita Beckman,
newly arrived in Todd's town from Los Angeles. But when
Todd's soccer teammate Randy starts spreading the rumor that
Rita's twin brother Alex is gay, Todd isn't sure he has the
courage to stick up for Alex.

THE HATE CRIME
by Phyllis Karas   78214-6/$3.99 US/$4.99 Can
Zack's dad is the district attorney, so Zack hears about all
kinds of terrible crimes. The latest case is about graffiti defac-
ing the local temple. But it's only when Zack tries to get to the
bottom of this senseless act that he fully understands the terror
these vicious scrawls evoke.